The Ladies of Whitechapel

Denise Bloom

www.darkstroke.com

Copyright © 2020 by Denise Bloom
Photography: Adobe Stock © Andrey Kiselev
Cover Design: Soqoqo
All rights reserved.

No part of this book may be used or reproduced in any manner whatsoever without written permission of the author or Crooked Cat/darkstroke except for brief quotations used for promotion or in reviews. This is a work of fiction. Names, characters, places, and incidents are used fictitiously. Any resemblance to actual persons living or dead, business establishments, events, or locales, is entirely coincidental.

First Dark Edition, darkstroke. 2020

Discover us online:
www.darkstroke.com

Find us on instagram:
www.instagram.com/darkstrokebooks

Include **#darkstroke** in a photo of yourself holding his book on Instagram and **something nice will happen.**

This book is dedicated to my wonderful late father, Fred Mapp, 1927-2018.

He sparked my imagination by reading bedtime stories from Edgar Allen Poe.

Acknowledgements

Thanks to all.

I would like to thank Laurence and Stephanie Patterson @darkstroke for their patience, guidance and support through the journey of producing a book, and Angela Wren (author) for her support. Thanks, also, to The Writers Cramp creative writing group, who have kept me amused in difficult times, and to Vanessa who hid her face when I read out the gory details.

And the last person but not the least must be my husband Peter, who makes me think of murder every day.

About the Author

Denise Bloom is a retired women's services manager. Running hostels, refuges and outreach domestic violence services across Yorkshire and Humberside. She now writes full time along with inspiring other in creative writing classes.

Through her love of Victorian England and Ripperology, a book was a natural step, using her knowledge of women's struggles in gruelling situations. This enables her to breathe life into her characters and allows the reader to experience the brutal life that women had to bear in the harsh streets of London Whitechapel 1888.

An author's note is included at the end of the stories.

The Ladies of Whitechapel

Emma Smith

Chapter One

A shrill scream filled the grand halls of Rushworth Manor. It was as if she knew what was to become of her. Victoria Charlotte Elizabeth Rushworth was born May the third 1843 and named after the new Queen. She had almost the same luxuries and comforts. Rushworth Manor was one of the grandest homes in Bradford, Yorkshire, set among rambling moors close to the River Aire. There were more than a dozen tenanted farms in the nearby district owned by the Rushworth family, as well as woollen mills in Keighley and Manningham. Over two-hundred were employed at the coal mine and iron ore mine in Low Moor. The Rushworths were well known and revered as good masters. They provided the best coal and fuel to power the giant machines that ran industrial England.

Victoria was a lucky child, the youngest of four. Her brothers had been sent away to school by the age of eight. She had her own governess and was permitted to stay at home with her mother and father. Her parents doted on her. Every day, when afternoon tea was cleared away, she performed for them, or for any guests that were there. She was proficient at the pianoforte from an early age and would recite poetry or sing a popular hymn. Her audience would clap politely as the elegant child shone a smile that would melt any heart.

Her brothers came home from school in the summer and at Christmas. They played games together in the gardens and woods surrounding the manor. While the boys' futures were already mapped out, Victoria often wondered what would happen to her. Charles, the eldest, was to leave school and would join the family firm, working his way through each department, then taking his place on the Board of Directors, eventually procuring his father's position as Chairman. James, the second brother, would join the army as an Officer and later become a Member of Parliament like her Uncle Charles. William, the youngest, would go to Edinburgh University to study medicine, and then who knows what? Victoria's fate, on the other hand, might be that of most young women of her class, to become a lady, to marry someone of the same standing, and to produce heirs for the family. She was spoiled, though it didn't spoil her nature. She was gentle, generous and kind and enjoyed the company of others, although her mother would say that she smiled too much for a gentlewoman.

As she grew, she became more beautiful. Her hair curled naturally and shone like golden hay. She was very popular at social events and often played the pianoforte when encouraged. She spoke French, wrote poetry, was a vociferous reader and had mastered watercolours. In fact, she would be a great catch for any wealthy landowner in the country. Her father said, as she grew up, that many men had discussed with him the possibility of her marrying their sons. There would be many suitors. But he insisted on being choosy. It had to be a good match as the Rushworth's dowry would be a somewhat healthy one.

Victoria's early years had been quiet. She had played around the grounds, happy with the freedom it gave her. Social events became a normal occurrence when she became sixteen. She visited neighbours for high tea or went with her mother and father to formal dinners. Most weeks she would go with her mother to nearby Harrogate to take the waters at the spa or to shop in the city of Leeds. Victoria had to have the latest fashions. But her father couldn't understand why a young girl had to have more than one hat as she only had one head. She would parade the purchase for him, and he would tut, then smile, as she glowed so full of life. Victoria would tell him that everything was an investment. If he wanted her to catch the best husband, she had to look her best.

It was a day in April 1860 that changed Victoria's life forever. A shopping trip was arranged to buy a corset for her up-coming birthday. She was to have a grand ball in her honour. The carriage was called for and both mother and daughter were assisted aboard by the Groomsman, Bill. The groom leant forward.

"Excuse me ma'am," he said quietly to her mother. "But we have a new boy on our journey today. His name is Joseph. He's my sister's lad."

Just as he was talked about, the tall, dark-haired youth bowed to both women. He wore the tunic of Rushworth Manor well, a dark blue woollen coat with dark trousers. Mrs Rushworth looked the boy up and down and nodded her approval. Victoria smiled one of her special smiles at the boy. The young man smiled back.

"Come on," the Groomsman said to the boy, and cuffed him across the ear.

Victoria bowed her head. She didn't want to get the poor lad into more trouble.

The trip was a success. After much searching, both ladies found corsets and feathers to their liking. On to the spa for the taking of waters. Victoria shot a quick look under her thick lashes at the handsome groom as he assisted the women back into the carriage. Victoria didn't understand the feeling in her stomach, tumbling over and over, making her want to swoon.

"Are you quite well Victoria? You have gone very pale."

Victoria could not tell her mother that she thought she had felt the first pain of love. It would never do. She rested her head on the side of the carriage and tried not to think of the boy.

Chapter Two

Victoria wasn't a confident horse-rider. She thought that the beast might just gallop away with her. But on Sunday, after church, she felt brave. A message was sent to the stables to prepare Chestnut, her brown mare.

"Well that's a treat for the horse. It will do you good," said her father.

She smiled. He wouldn't have approved if he'd known the reason she wanted to ride.

Victoria took great care in the way she dressed, her hair cocooned into a small black riding net. She checked herself in the mirror and smiled at the reflection.

Bill had been told Victoria would be riding that day, but it was Joseph that was ordered to saddle the mare and to accompany his young mistress on her ride. Victoria stood in the yard with a confident air. Joseph had already taken the horse from its stable and saddled it. He wasn't very happy. Sunday was his first day off since he began working and, as did everyone, he considered it his rest day. Bill had said the family rarely rode, so here he was, the very first Sunday, having to look after the daughter. He hoped she wouldn't be making a habit of it. He didn't think it was her fault. It was obvious to him that she was spoiled.

He took another look at her. He thought that she was, perhaps, sixteen or seventeen. She was very beautiful, and her smile was as brilliant as the sunshine. She was bold, staring directly back at him.

"I can get on myself, Joseph." She declined his cupped hands and chose to walk to the mounting steps. Her side-saddle made her look straight and proud. Joseph stood back.

"Would you like me to accompany you, ma'am?" His voice was strong. She didn't frighten him.

"Yes, I think that would be a good idea. I haven't ridden for a few months. I only want to go as far as the river." Her voice was cultured, far from the broad Yorkshire of his own. Joseph had saddled another mare in case he had to join her. He jumped artistically into the saddle and followed his mistress into the long meadow. Victoria trotted silently through the tall sweet-smelling grass to the River Aire. She dismounted, taking in the beauty of her surroundings. Joseph sat on his horse, respectfully, a little way from her. She wore a magnificent coat of dark blue velvet.

Victoria walked slowly to the river's edge. She stumbled on an uneven piece of ground and, as quick as a flash, Joseph jumped down from the saddle.

"Ma'am you must be careful. There are rat holes and rabbit holes near the river."

She steadied herself on his outstretched arm. Victoria could feel the muscles flex under his shirt.

"Thank you, Joseph. You're very kind."

He guided her back to Chestnut and they rode side-by-side on their way back to the manor.

"I know you live at the Manor now, Joseph, but where do you call home?" Her head was tilted. She listened eagerly to his words.

"Wrose, ma'am. It's near Shipley."

"And do you have family there?"

"Just my mother. My two sisters are in service in York. My father is dead, almost two years now." She felt sad for this young man, with the broad shoulders and handsome face.

"Does your mother miss you? I am sure she must."

"Yes, but we have to work. My mother is in the mill, but I'm more of an outdoor person. I couldn't be locked up in a building. It doesn't seem natural."

Victoria nodded. He had sense and he was real. He

smelled of the heather, of the moors and looked like he belonged in the country. Not like the suitors that were paraded in front of her at the social events she frequented.

"I hope you enjoy your employment here with my family."

They trotted slowly into the stable yard. Joseph had enjoyed the ride.

***

Victoria found herself choosing to ride every day in the coming weeks. She always asked Joseph to accompany her.

The head groom, Bill, started to become concerned. "You're spending a lot of time with the young mistress, lad," he said. "Be careful. She's not in your class. And if the master finds out you will be for the high jump."

"It's my job, Bill. She asks for me. We're friends."

"Friends? Don't be an idiot. Lads from your place don't get to be friends with the likes of her."

Bill pulled the saddle from the mare. Joseph felt his face redden. He wasn't an idiot. Why couldn't a man from his class be friends with whoever they wanted to be? He knew that he loved Victoria, but understood it was wrong. When they were together, they seemed to talk on the same level. She was clever. She had experienced things he never had or ever would get the chance to.

On the following Saturday it was Victoria's birthday. She was to have a grand ball at home. The local gentry and influential dignitaries were invited. Victoria thought it was more like a cattle market and that she might be the prize cow, to be engaged to be married to a suitable gentleman who could provide her with the comforts of modern living. She had been fitted with a new ball gown of a delicate blue; her tiny waist encapsulated in a boned corset. Earlier that morning she had decided to go riding to free her mind of the ball, and had to see Joseph again.

They rode side by side into long meadow. They reached the old oak tree near the river, and Victoria dismounted and walked to the river's edge.

"Excuse me, ma'am. I know it's your birthday today, and I hoped that you might accept this. I know it is not usual for a groom to give gifts." His face was now the colour of beetroot. He held a small silver locket on a silver chain.

"I told you to call me Victoria when we are alone, Joseph." She took the locket from him. "You shouldn't have done this. It's beautiful. But I didn't expect anything from you. It looks very expensive."

"It was my grandmother's. There isn't anyone else in the world I would give it to." He stepped a little closer to Victoria. She handed the locket to him, an indication that she wanted him to put the locket around her neck. His hands trembled, and his long fingers brushed the skin at the back of her neck. When fastened, she turned a little too quickly and their eyes met. Joseph bent his head and kissed Victoria very softly, with a passion that rose through their bodies. The kiss echoed Victoria's feelings. They had both wanted it to happen and both enjoyed the pleasure. Victoria had never been kissed before, but her heart was bursting. It was true love. He wasn't one of the elegant beaus that stood lounging in her drawing room. This was a real man, one who loved her, not her father's money.

"I must see you again, Victoria." He kissed her hair and neck. She felt dizzy, and confused, and frightened and angry. She felt every possible emotion, her mind was a mess of conflicting thoughts. Her parents would be angry, but she loved Joseph. There was no going back. She was melting into his strong arms. Suddenly she came to her senses and pushed him away gently.

"Stop, Joseph. Yes, after the ball tonight I will meet you by the greenhouse. It will be after eleven." Joseph agreed and said he would be waiting.

It took Victoria's maid, Emma, four hours to prepare Victoria, with the bathing, hair dressing, face powdering and corset pulling. Victoria's mother and father were proud of their beautiful daughter. She was the catch of the century. There would be many gentlemen in her father's study tonight drinking brandy and smoking his best cigars. And they would discuss a joining of family dynasties.

Victoria descended the staircase, and the partygoers applauded the young women with admiration. The young men waited eagerly, hoping to sign her dance card. The older men were trying to add up how much money she would be worth. Victoria was only thinking of Joseph's kiss. It still lingered on her lips. The throng below didn't mean anything. Joseph had been told to assist at the ball and was dressed appropriately to take hats and capes from the guests. He was positioned at the bottom of the great staircase when Victoria appeared like an angel in blue. He had never seen anyone more beautiful. She glided down every step, her smile lighting every corner of the room. Victoria's feet ached as she was whirled around for almost every dance. On one occasion she had to beg Edward Drysdale to allow her to sit for a drink of water because she was so hot. Her corset didn't allow too much time for relaxing, so she was up in a little more than a breath.

Carriages were at eleven and, by eleven-thirty, all the guests had left. Victoria went to her mother and father, who were both in her father's study. She wanted to thank them and to tell them she was to retire. She embraced her parents and expressed her gratitude for the beautiful cream ivory pearls that were almost the same colour as her skin. Her father sat in a high-backed leather chair, puffed up with pride and satisfaction. Her mother, on the other hand, looked very nervous.

"I have some good news. Yes, good news indeed." He puffed heavily on his Cuban cigar. Her mother gave a short cough. Victoria moved from one foot to the other, her shoes pinching her toes.

"Your future is set, and what a rosy one it will be. You will be the richest woman in Yorkshire. You will have servants waiting on your every need. You will travel the world. I am so happy for you, my daughter. We are so proud of you." He was satisfied he had done the best deal for her. Victoria couldn't speak at first, but summoned the courage to break the uncomfortable silence.

"Who is it, father?" she whispered, her world falling apart before her.

"It will be a wonderful coupling. You will make a beautiful bride and, I'm sure, a wonderful mother."

"Father, who am I to marry?" Her mother shifted her seating position.

"George Hardcastle. His father is Francis Hardcastle. He owns the mill in Saltaire and they own land across North Yorkshire. He has been to Oxford so intelligent, and he will be able to converse with you on many subjects. I thought you would like that. He likes music, another of your loves. A perfect match."

He waited to see the excitement in her eyes, but it didn't appear. Victoria's brain was swirling, her feet were throbbing. How could her father think she would be interested in George Hardcastle? He was ten years older, overweight and short. He wasn't Victoria's knight in shining armour. She could see that her mother didn't approve of the match, but she knew her father's decision was final.

"I'll speak to you at length tomorrow girl. Off to bed. I expect you are tired." He sounded, to her at least, a little annoyed that she was not in raptures at the choice of suitor.

Victoria left the room and ran straight to the back door that led out to the gardens. The moonlight allowed her to get to the greenhouse without any further injury to her worn feet. Joseph had eagerly been waiting for her. She was wrapped into his arms in a second, and they kissed with passion. The scent of the thyme and rosemary filled the air about them. Victoria buried her head into Joseph's shirt and started to cry.

"What's all this, lass? What is it my love?" He lifted her chin. She looked into his eyes, the eyes she loved.

"I am to be married," she whispered.

Joseph was astonished. "Married? Who is it?"

"George Hardcastle. He is a pig and he looks like one." They both laughed.

"I can't marry him now, Joseph. I just can't."

"It is expected that you marry him, Victoria. Your parents expect you to do your duty."

"Please save me, Joseph. My darling Joe. I love you. I can't marry him."

She had said what Joseph wanted to hear.

"I love you, Victoria. I will do anything for you, but I am not a rich man. You live a different life to me."

Victoria stood away from him.

"I don't care about riches, I love you."

"I will go to your father. I will tell him we are in love."

"He will kill you, Joseph. You don't know my father. He won't allow it." They moved to the wooden bench in the greenhouse. Joseph wiped away dead leaves and they sat together to work out the problem. He dabbed away the tears from her cheek with a crisp linen handkerchief. They kissed gently to blot out the thoughts of parents.

He held her close. "I will do anything your father asks of me. I could work in the mill so I could earn more money. I don't want to let you go, Victoria."

"I don't want to leave your side ever. I love you, Joseph."

The two young people were lost in each other's arms, defying all status and standing. Joseph's hands covered every part of Victoria's body. It was too late now. She couldn't marry anyone else. She was Joseph's. She had given herself to him with passion and no remorse. Victoria couldn't imagine anyone else in her life. She didn't care anymore about what her mother or father thought. She was going to marry Joseph and, if they didn't like it, she would live in a cottage and have his children and be blissfully happy with her man until the end of her days.

Chapter Three

On Sunday morning after breakfast the family sat quietly in the small salon. Bill the groom was escorted into the room by the butler.

"Sir, Bill needs to speak with you. It's important."

Victoria was worried. Bill's face was hard, and he held his cap in his gnarled hand.

"Sir, I hoped you might allow young Joseph to go home. His mother has passed away and the family need him to arrange the funeral. I would like to ask for some time off also, to say goodbye to my sister." Victoria's father agreed that Joseph should be allowed to go to the family home. He would be expected to return the following week and, when the funeral was arranged, Bill could take an hour or two to attend. The groom bowed and told his master that he was very generous. As Bill left, Victoria's father shouted for the butler to return.

"Mathers, when has it been my duty to deal with stable hands and their problems? It would have been more appropriate for Mrs Sykes to conduct the interview."

"Sorry sir."

Mathers bowed his head and left.

Victoria wondered how Joseph was. She wanted to take him into her arms and console him. She left the room and ran to the stables, hoping to find Joe. The lad was sweeping the yard before he left for home.

"Oh, Joseph. I'm so sorry to hear of your mother's

passing."

"Victoria." His voice was husky, he held her close, but they jumped apart when Bill shouted across the yard. He shook his head as he walked towards the couple.

"Ma'am, you need to return to the house." Victoria bent her head and did as she was told. She hoped that Bill would not report back to her father.

"You are a young fool. What did I tell you? You're finished here." Bill spoke through clenched teeth.

"You've lost your job and you have put mine in jeopardy. Don't imagine the family will allow this to go on. They won't. You're nowt but a peasant to them."

"We love each other, Bill. It's real. It doesn't matter what class we are."

"It does matter. They are the masters. We are the ones that serve. Your master has allowed you to go for a week because he is a good master. You have betrayed him. I suggest that you look for another job in that week and give notice. All I can say is that it is a good thing your mother is dead. She won't have this shame put on her."

He walked away from his nephew, still muttering about family values. Joseph couldn't leave Victoria but knew that Bill was right, he had to go. The funeral was held on the following Thursday at ten in the morning. A few neighbours attended the service in the Wesleyan Chapel on Wrose Road. Joseph's sisters sobbed throughout the service. Joseph stood grim-faced. His world had crumbled all within a week. The family trod through puddles to the graveyard and, to add to the sorry sight, the heavens opened, and rain began to fall once again. Bill moved forward and touched Joseph's shoulder to offer some comfort. Tears that had welled in his eyes now fell easily. His sisters gathered around him and they all wept together. Joseph lifted his head to gasp a breath of air. It was then that he caught sight of Victoria, stood by a willow tree, dressed in a black topcoat and black hat. She bowed her head.

The sisters were led away by Bill, and Victoria approached, taking hold of Joseph's hands.

"I am so sorry for your loss. I had to come."

"You shouldn't have. Bill says he might lose his job if your father finds out about us. I can't do that to him. You need to go back to your family." He couldn't look her in the face.

"No, Joseph. I love you. Don't you understand? They will make me marry George Hardcastle. Do you want that?"

"You know I love you. The thought of another man being with you breaks my heart and fills me with fury. But we are not meant to be together. We come from two different ways of life."

"I'll go to my father and tell him I want to be with you." Joseph was shocked that she would do that for him.

"Please, Joseph. I love you." She kissed him hard and he responded.

"No, I will go to your father if you are sure this is what you want. I'm not a rich man. You'll not have the luxuries you do now." She nodded as hot salty tears ran down her face.

***

The next morning Victoria went down to breakfast. Her heart raced and she was unable to contain the nervous excitement that ran through her body. She couldn't eat the poached egg, instead pushing it to one side of her plate. Her mother remarked that she looked flushed and asked of her health.

"No, mother. I am well. Just not hungry."

"You're excited about your engagement my dear," her father contributed.

***

They sat after their meal in the morning room. Her father read his newspaper, her mother at her writing desk with her letters. Victoria had a piece of needlework on her lap when Mathers entered.

"I am sorry to interrupt, Sir, but I have the groom, young Joseph from the stables. He wishes to speak to you. I've said that you are engaged, but he insists that there is a problem with Miss Rushworth."

Her mother and father both looked across the room at Victoria who turned a brilliant shade of beetroot red.

"The blaggard. How dare he come to our door? He needs to speak with Bill. What's all this about Victoria, do you know?"

Victoria shook her head.

"Who the hell does he think he is?"

"Shall I send him away, Sir?"

"Yes, I don't have time for grooms. Send him to Bill." The butler was dismissed.

Victoria held her head down. She could feel her mother's eyes on her face. There were raised voices from the hallway, then the doors to the morning room flew open.

"What?" Her father turned in his chair. In front of them, with Mathers pulling on his arm, was Joseph.

"Sir, it is important. I need to speak to you urgently," Joseph panted.

"You are an oaf man. You are a fool. What are you doing here? You're relieved of your duties. I can't have servants making scenes in my house, in front of my wife and daughter." Her father stood up to his full height, every inch a nobleman.

"I love your daughter, sir, and she is in love with me. I want to ask for her hand in marriage." It tumbled out. He had said what he had been practicing all night. Victoria had hidden her face. She couldn't look at her father or her mother.

"How dare you. My daughter is engaged to be married and to someone that has class and money, not a wastrel such as you."

"It's true, father. I love Joseph." The quiet soft voice cut through the atmosphere. All eyes turned towards the young girl. Her father stood with his mouth wide open, her mother held her handkerchief to her face and Mathers let go of his prisoner. Joseph moved towards Victoria and they held hands.

"I will not have it, you fool. This is not what is going to happen. You will be thrown from my property and you will not come within ten miles of my daughter."

"Father, I love Joseph."

"So this is why you have taken up riding on such frequent occasions. I thought I had brought you up better than this. What has love got to do with marriage?"

Victoria had never seen her father so angry. His face was red, and she imagined steam coming from his ears.

"Get out of my house. Mathers, get the other men."

Her mother sobbed loudly. A moment later, in marched two gardeners, a kitchen boy and a pantry boy. Joseph struggled with them as they attempted to remove him from the morning room.

"You, my girl, will not be out of our sights until your marriage. I am not having any of this love in my house. You have a duty to us as parents and to the rest of the family. Love indeed." He left the room to go to his study. He needed a large brandy. Daughters, he was lucky he only had one.

Victoria turned to her mother. Surely she would know how she felt, but she appeared just as angry as her father and turned away.

"You need to go to your room and stay there until dinner. Your father may have calmed down a little then. How could you have done this to us? You've had everything anyone could ever want in their life."

Victoria left the room sobbing and shut herself in her bed chamber. What would she do without her love? He was everything to her.

***

It was almost two o'clock when Victoria looked at her bedside clock. She heard pebbles at the window. On looking out, she saw a dark handsome man, her Joe was waving excitedly from below. Victoria opened the window and waved back. Joe then put a set of ladders against the ivy and climbed, like Romeo, into her bed chamber. They embraced and Victoria whispered how she had missed him.

"Shush, my love. I have come for you. Do you want to be with me forever? If you do, come with me now. I will not be able to give you all the things you have here. I am a poor man but I'm strong I can work, and I love you."

"And I love you, Joseph. I don't care about all the frippery. I want to be loved by you. I want to spend the rest of my life with you." They kissed again.

"You can only take a few things. Pack the essentials. We will have to move quickly." Victoria ran around the room picking things up, discarding them, then picking them up again. She put a nightdress and some underclothes into her carpet bag. She didn't bother with the whale-boned corset. That was one thing she wouldn't miss. She packed her hairbrush with the silver handle, lavender toilet water and the pearl necklace her parents had bought for her birthday. In the top drawer of the tall boy was her silk purse with two five-pound notes that had been sent by a distant aunt. The money would be crucial in the weeks before Joseph could work. Joseph helped her down the ladder, and they ran hand-in-hand across the long meadow, the sound of dogs barking from the nearby farm. However, no-one came to find out what was causing the disturbance. After walking along the riverbank, they came across a barn filled with fresh hay. The exhausted couple collapsed in each other's arms, sleeping contented.

Chapter Four

The sun woke the chickens in the farmyard and Victoria turned towards Joseph. He was still asleep. She gently touched his face, tracing the outline of his square jaw. She had never slept outside before. It was very uncomfortable. Victoria stretched out her bones. Still aching, she bent down and kissed Joseph's full lips. The lips turned into a smile and kissed her back.

"Now then my lady, I need to provide you with breakfast. Come on."

They walked a little further until they reached a village. A baker's shop had just opened the door and the smell of fresh bread filled the air. They ate chunks of bread and fat rascals. Victoria thought she was dinning on caviar, it tasted so good.

"We will go to London, then we will find somewhere to live. I'll get a job and you'll have your own palace." Joseph was excited.

Victoria had placed the two five-pound notes in his hand. He was the man and needed to care for her. Joseph had stared at the large five-pound notes for almost ten minutes. He had never seen so much money. They wouldn't be short of somewhere to live or be hungry. The money would last for months.

"I'm happy wherever you are." She smiled at him, not caring what was to become of them. They were young and fit. At the stockyard, Joseph went into the office and came back with good news, a wagon and horses were going to

Birmingham and then onto London that afternoon. The fare was two shillings each. The gaffer in the yard was not sure about the couple and was extremely surprised at the presentation of a five-pound note to pay the fare. He thought that the lad seemed to be a local, but the young woman had leather boots and quality clothes. Who was he to turn away good money? That afternoon they were hauled aboard the wagon and sat, not very comfortably, among barrels and sacks. Victoria was excited. The four shire horses jolted the wagon as they pulled away. She wondered what her father would say. She should have left a note, but she didn't have the time. When they were settled, she would write a letter and let them know she was safe and well.

***

It was dark when they reached the inn near Birmingham. Joseph had rented a room and they ate a supper of boiled beef and dumplings before falling into their soft bed. After their lovemaking, they held each other tightly, hoping for life to treat them gently. The next morning, they were woken by the wagon driver banging on their door. He told them that he would leave them there if they weren't down in five minutes.

Three minutes later they were sat among the barrels, laughing at the driver who was swearing profanities at them both.

***

As dusk approached, they arrived in London. Joseph was in awe as the buildings grew before them. He had never been out of Yorkshire nor seen so many people. Victoria had been on several occasions, usually to visit her Uncle Charles who lived in Whitehall, but never on the back of a wagon among barrels of beer. They rented a room at a hostelry near the delivery depot and ate in the inn's dining room. The food wasn't very good, but they didn't care. They laughed and drank beer, then made love in the horsehair bed.

***

They sat in the morning, looking out of the window at the buildings and chimneys, with smoke spewing out from them. People were rushing down the road and there was a woman selling pies from a barrow on the corner of the street.

They found a house agent who took them to see a property on Hope Street. It was part of a large terrace. Their portion was a front parlour, a back kitchen with range and a bedroom upstairs. There was a back yard with a shared privy. Victoria realised they could not afford a large house and London prices were high, as the agent insisted on repeating to them. She wandered through the shabby rooms. It wasn't what she had imagined but, with a little touch from a woman, the place would soon be bright, and she was, at least, mistress of her own home. The rent included a scuttle of coal and gas lighting. They shopped for bed linen, plates and crockery.

***

Victoria wasn't a cook and it took some weeks before she was able to put a decent meal on the table. It was not long before Joseph had secured a job in the local farriers. It wasn't good pay, but it was a start. Victoria washed down the walls and scrubbed the floors. She bought material for curtains and made the home look inviting. The harsh soap made her hands rough, but this was what she had signed up for to be with Joseph. Two months had gone by and the couple enjoyed the freedom of London town. They would take walks in the park on a Sunday and Joseph would take her to Buckingham Palace to stare through the gates, hoping to see the Queen. Victoria loved the way Joseph wanted her to link his arm. He looked so handsome. She was proud to be at his side.

Chapter Five

Victoria stepped off the pavement just avoiding a wagon and horses. Carts rumbled on the cobble stones before her and the street sellers proclaimed their wares. London was alive, compared to Bradford, anyway.

A young ragged boy stood on the corner of the street yelling at the top of his voice. "Come and get your news. Come and get your news. Read all about it. Heiress abducted by groom. Read all about it."

Victoria's heart stopped just for a second. She felt into the pocket of her apron and found the farthing she needed. She didn't look at anyone that passed her in the street but rushed, her feet barely touching the cobbles. At home she spread the paper onto the kitchen table. The headlines read that a Yorkshire heiress had been abducted from her home by a groom who had been working on the family's farm. The Honourable Victoria Rushworth, daughter of Sir William Rushworth had disappeared from the family home in Bradford, West Yorkshire. The family were devastated. Miss Rushworth was also the niece of Sir Charles Foster member of Parliament.

Victoria didn't know what to do. They hadn't met many people, so didn't have any friends. The neighbours, who Victoria only acknowledged with a nod, knew her as Mrs Turner, wife of Joseph. When Joe came in from ·work, smelling of manure, Victoria showed him the newspaper. He told her not to worry. It was only to be expected that her parents would look for her.

He looked into her eyes. "Do you want to go home, Victoria?"

"No, of course not. I want to be at your side. Even though it is a very smelly side now. Let's get the bath in."

Joseph went to the yard with a smile of satisfaction and carried the tin bath into the kitchen. There were two large pans of water heating on the kitchen range. He undressed as Victoria watched, his body still moist from the sweat that had clung to his vest. He sat with legs bent, squeezing his body into the tiny zinc bath. She poured warm water over him, and he sighed with pleasure. With a small brush she scrubbed his back, removing the grime and the smell from his muscled frame.

"Come join me." He tried to pull her into the tub. Victoria screamed and ran to the safety of the parlour. She was happy, blissfully happy, there was no way she could go home and marry George Hardcastle.

***

They ate a supper of oxtail stew with chunks of bread. Victoria had become an imaginative cook, and Joseph was pleased. The first few weeks had been dire with strange concoctions presented to him on a plate.

"What if the neighbours find out about us? We all live on top of each other. They may hear you calling me Victoria."

Joseph thought about it. They agreed that Victoria would be called Emma. It was Joseph's grandmother's name, so was fitting for his other love. Emma touched the locket, yes, that was excellent.

***

It was difficult for a few weeks, but the name seemed to suit her and soon the neighbours she had been friendly towards were calling her by her first name, Emma. It was at that time that Joseph had brought someone home that he had met in the tavern. His name was Michael. He had been in

London for two years, originally from York.

"Emma, this is my friend, Michael. I told you about him. Michael, this is my Emma." Emma curtsied as Joseph winked at her.

"You said she was a beauty, Joseph. But I didn't realise she would be so beautiful. Nice to meet you Mrs Turner. Joseph is a very lucky man."

"Thank you, sir. It's good to meet Joseph's friends."

"Oh, my gawd you've got a plum in your mouth. You aren't from Yorkshire."

"She was in a convent." Said Joseph. "She wasn't allowed out, put in there by her family. I helped her escape." Michael nodded, not quite believing the story Joe was giving him, but who cared? This was London. Everyone had a story.

Michael gave a large bow. "Your majesty." They all laughed.

Emma thought she would have to be careful of her manners, it would give her game away if she used the refined manners of her class. She had to blend into the community.

"Michael says that there is a lot of building going on in the town and there are good jobs for those who aren't afraid of work, twice the wages I am on now."

He waited eagerly for Emma's response.

"That's wonderful, Joe. What would you be doing?" Michael had to snigger again at Emma's accent. It seemed so strange coming from the young girl.

"It just needs a couple of good handshakes and you're on," Michael added.

When Michael had gone, she asked what a couple of good handshakes meant. Joseph laughed at her naivety.

"I meant that if I pay for a couple of ales to the gaffer, he will take me on."

Emma had learnt another lesson. Growing up in this new life was as though she had been born again. Her new home was clean with dainty curtains to the windows. They had acquired two comfy armchairs that had been covered with new material. One day, as she swept the wooden floor, she felt a little dizzy, so she sat for a time and the feeling passed.

Then from nowhere her stomach retched. She ran to the outside lavatory, just managing to reach the wooden seat. Her next-door neighbour had heard the poor young woman's cries. Mrs Capstick was big and round with bosoms boiling over the top of her cotton blouse.

"Now then, Mrs Turner. You not well?" She had a quick look around the scrubbed-out lavatory and was impressed at the cleanliness.

Emma sat on the floor, exhausted by her sickness.

"I feel so dizzy. I must have a chill." She felt her brow that was cold and damp. Mrs Capstick burst out laughing, a loud deep sound making Emma cover her ears.

"You don't have a chill my dear. You are with child." She giggled again. "I've had seven of me own. I knows the signs. You are definitely with child."

She helped Emma up and went with her to the backdoor. Emma allowed the woman to follow her into the kitchen.

"I will make you some tea. Where is it?" She had a good look around the kitchen. It was neat and well looked after. Mrs Capstick had not had much to do with her neighbour, but she had said good morning on a few occasions. She thought that the young woman had manners and spoke very well for the usual inhabitants of Hope Street. Emma pointed to the cupboard above the kitchen range. Tea was made and the two women spoke about babies. Emma felt that she had found her first friend. Mrs Capstick was a middle-aged woman. She was friendly and knowledgeable of women's things and Victoria thought she would need the help as her pregnancy developed. When Joseph came home that evening, she wasn't sure how to tell him. She had made him his favourite pie of steak and oyster. Victoria had become adept at making pastry and Joseph encouraged his young wife praising her attempts at cooking. After his scrub in the tin bath they sat down together to eat the golden pie.

"I'm so proud of you. This is delicious, but there is something wrong. What is it?"

She was shocked that he knew her so well. She stared at the floor, then extending her arms over the table, she held his hands.

"I'm having a baby, Joseph."

Joe stood up and twirled his beautiful girl around. They kissed, and Joseph set her down and touched her stomach. Emma was pleased that he had the same feelings. They had little money, and this would be another strain on the finances.

***

In bed that night Joseph stroked her stomach, and they thought of names for boys and girls. Joseph wanted a boy, someone to carry his name on. He wondered if Emma's family might allow her back into the fold if they had a grandchild. Emma wasn't too sure.

***

The pregnancy went well. For the first four months she retched every day at the most inconvenient times. She had a problem when shopping at the markets, and the fish sellers' barrow would send her immediately to a corner to dispose of her breakfast. She had to buy clothes from the local pawnbrokers to cover her expanding waistline. But this change also allowed her to blend into the community. Mrs Capstick had commented on the quality of her blouse. She now wore a full skirt with several muslin underskirts. Her top was of cotton and a shawl of wool was wrapped around her shoulders.

Chapter Six

The sound of church bells was deafening. Joseph ran into the road, and he could see that people were shouting. At first he was unable to hear what was being said.

Kitty Capstick stood on the front doorstep. "It's Prince Albert," she said. "He's dead. God bless his soul. Her majesty will be heartbroken." She sniffed into her apron.

Women were openly crying in the street. Joseph went back inside to tell Emma the news. She had made him a cup of tea. The nation mourned.

Emma had wrapped black crepe paper to the doorknobs and the curtains were drawn as marks of respect. The funeral was performed without the Queen as she was too distraught to attend. Factories closed for a dignified time. This included Joseph's work at the sugar refinery, which was closed for a week. Emma was sorry the Prince had died but it meant there was no money coming into the household. Emma thought hard at what they should do, then handed over her set of pearls to Joseph.

"No lass. They're yours."

"What do I need with pearls? We must have food in our stomachs and a roof over our heads."

Joseph said they needed to take the pearls to the pawnbrokers. The cobbled street was narrow and the pavement was full of hawkers selling their wares. Emma longed for an open field, for the moors of Yorkshire.

The sign creaked. The three gold balls swung in the

breeze. Joseph pushed the door to the sound of a tinkling bell in a far back room. The old man rubbed his hands as he met his first customers of the day.

"Yes sir, and madam. What can I do for you both today?" He rubbed his hands again, the two gold rings on his index finger glinting. Joseph open his pocket and lay the string of cream pearls onto the counter.

"My wife would like to sell her pearls."

The old man's face lit up. "Oh, they are fine, very fine."

He pulled a glass from his waistcoat pocket and put his eye to it, rolling each pearl in his grimy fingers. He then let his gaze fall onto Emma, she didn't look as though she could afford pearls.

"Where did you come by these, madam?" He squinted at her, still rolling the pearls in his fingers.

"My mother and father bought them from me sir, for my birthday." Emma stood tall as she spoke. Her voice was a shock to the old man. She had a cultured voice, certainly not a match for her clothes that were much the same as those he sold in his shop. His gaze returned to the pearls.

"I can give you two pounds for them."

He waited for the answer.

"Two pounds? They're worth thirty or forty times that amount," said Joseph.

Emma was angry at the amount offered.

"No, sir. We haven't stolen the pearls, they're mine to sell. Please, be an honest man."

"Three pounds and that is my last offer. I need to find a person to sell them to." He put the pearls onto the counter. With one swift movement, Emma retrieved the pearls. The pawnbroker took a step backwards. Even Joseph was shocked.

"You're not stealing my pearls. I don't think you're an honest man." Joseph loved her more at that moment, defiant, strong, she had principles. The old pawnbroker wanted the pearls and realised that he would have to pay a little more than he wanted to this fiery woman. Emma held them tightly in her small fist. The man tried not to look too anxious.

Joseph didn't say anything. The man nodded.

"All right. Every time it's the ladies that get me, every time. Five pounds and not a penny more."

It still wasn't enough, but Emma relented. The pearls had been the last link to her parents, and now they had gone. The man held his hands out and Emma reluctantly dropped the pearls into them. He curled his bony fingers around his new purchase and put them into his waistcoat pocket along with his eyeglass. He then dug deep into his outer coat pocket and produced a silk purse and from that he unfolded five pound notes. He passed them over to Joseph who folded them and gave them to Emma who put them in her purse.

***

The landlord's agent called that evening and took his ten shillings rent money for two weeks.

"Well, Mr Turner, this is most unusual. I have had many families falling short this week with the Prince's death and works closing. Most unusual. But I'm grateful. I'm sure Mr Brydon will be also. He's a good landlord to those who pays their dues."

He handed Joseph his change. The remainder of the money had been hidden in the tea caddy. Joseph went out and bought two pork pies and a quart of beer. They ate cheese and pickle with pork pie. A feast for the two of them. Emma was sad that she had parted with the pearls but was pleased that she could provide food and shelter for them. Joseph would be back to work the next week, so they would be able to pay the rent and have enough to eat. They were well off for a short while. It was to be hoped there were no more disasters.

Chapter Seven

Arthur was born on a Sunday. The church bells rang loud and clear as they welcomed the little boy. The frost had formed on the inside of the kitchen window, even though there was a fire burning in the kitchen range.

Joseph had been building an extension to the sugar refinery just off Old Montague Street in Whitechapel. Emma had been restless most of the night. Her waters had broken at breakfast time. She started to panic. She didn't know where the baby was going to come out or how it was going to come out. It was something her mother had never discussed with her and she didn't think it was correct to speak to Joseph about it. He made her tea and went next door to Kitty who had said she would help with the birthing.

"Oh, it's her first. It'll be a few hours yet. I'll call in about dinner time, but come for me if you need me earlier."

Joseph didn't think it would take so long. The sheep and horses he'd delivered in Yorkshire were there in a breath.

The heat started to fill the rooms slowly as Emma sipped her tea.

"I'm frightened Joseph," she said.

"My love, I am here. Kitty knows what she's doing."

He stroked her forehead as another pain caused her to groan. Just after midday, Kitty arrived at the kitchen door. Joseph took her through to the bedroom where Emma was crying with pain and fear.

"You need to boil some water and I will need some scissors and cloths."

Kitty had put a clean white apron over her stuff skirt. She smiled to Emma.

"You're doing well dearie. It's not long now." Kitty led Joseph out of the bedroom.

"It's not a place for men."

She closed the door behind him. Joe settled by the warmth of the kitchen range, waiting for his child to be born. It was two hours later when Joseph heard a piercing scream from Emma, then a shrill wail. Ten minutes later, Kitty Capstick emerged from the bedroom beaming proudly.

"It's a boy Mr Turner. Congratulations. Mother and son are both doing well."

Joseph went into the bedroom to find Emma sat up in bed holding a bundle of woollen shawl, a robust baby boy using his lungs as to what they were built for. Emma stroked the baby's face until the cries subsided. Joseph kissed her gently.

A few days later, Michael arrived with a bottle of brandy. He had bought it at the docks. He said it would be good for the mother and the baby. His wife swore by the brandy to soothe upset stomachs and any other ailment. He also had a cake made with almonds for the lovely mother. Emma thanked him. Michael had been a good friend to her and Joseph. He had shown them around London when they first became friends, took them to a tavern to experience their first taste of gin and wormwood wine. The bitter liquid was not something she would ever get used to. They had been with Michael and his wife, Mary to the music hall where they had watched jugglers and singers. Mary was a large woman a bit older than Emma. She was pleasant enough, but Emma thought she was someone she didn't want to associate with. Joseph would have been upset at her thoughts, but she didn't like her hanging on to Joseph's arm or the way she got drunk and then fall over. It was when they were drinking and having fun that Michael would make smart remarks about Emma's accent. Mary thought Emma was toffee nosed, and she needed to be brought down a peg or two. She joined in the fun mimicking Emma.

They couldn't all go out now as they had a little one to

look after and, although Joseph was an attentive father, he had started to go for a drink to the Ten Bells near work with the other men. It was money they hadn't got, and the money that had been saved had been broken into on many occasions.

Chapter Eight
1868

A year passed quickly. Joseph still worked long hours at the sugar refinery to make sure they had enough money to live. Arthur was a fine boy, healthy and alert. As a family they thrived. Each Sunday they would walk to the park, Joseph carrying his young son on his shoulders. They would eat chestnuts or baked potatoes, from the sellers close by. Emma was happy but missed her family. She thought that they should know of their grandchild and wrote a letter in her best handwriting, explaining her parents were now grandparents, and that the child was healthy and that they were all well. She hoped they were of a healthy disposition. Emma took the letter to Old Cavendish Street Post Office for delivery.

***

Three months went by with no answer. She had to resign herself to the fact that this was her family, Joseph and little Arthur.

***

Time passed and life was good to them. Arthur was healthy, which was wonderful as many children were malnourished and sick. The area was rife with unknown diseases from the river, and the streets were filled with human and animal waste. On Arthur's second birthday Emma's life was turned upside down. In the afternoon she was sitting at the kitchen table, sewing a button onto Joseph's Sunday shirt. Arthur was asleep on the bed. There was a knock to the door and Michael walked into the kitchen, he held his cap in his hand and stared at the floor.

"What's wrong? Where's Joseph?" She put her sewing down. Her head started to spin. She knew something dreadful had happened.

"I was working with Joseph on the roof of the new part of the sugar refinery. He got his foot stuck in the gutter. He didn't have a chance, Emma. I'm sorry. He's gone."

Emma's mouth was open. She let out a wail like a wounded animal. She fell into a heap on the kitchen floor. Michael helped her up. Arthur had been awoken in the bedroom and she went to fetch him, drying her eyes with her apron.

"Where have they taken him, Michael?"

"The workhouse mortuary on Old Montague Street."

It was as though he was embarrassed to say the words. The workhouse was the most feared place for people at the bottom of the chain. Families were split up into accommodation for women, children and men. Food was dished out three times a day in return for work. The food was usually dripping and bread, or gruel with little meat or vegetables. The mortuary was for the dead of the workhouse, or those who were not able to pay for a better place to lay their bones.

"The gaffer gave me this for you, and the lads gave me a few shillings to help bury him."

He laid the ten-shilling note and the coins on the table. This was all Joseph was worth.

Emma took Arthur to Kitty's and explained quickly what had happened. The poor woman shrieked the street down then lifted little Arthur up and planted him on her great bosom.

"The poor mite," she cried.

Emma tidied her hair. She brushed her Sunday dress and tried to make herself presentable. She took the omnibus to Old Montague Street. Immediately facing the stop was a building painted a dark blue. The word 'women' was chiselled in the stone above the door. Further along the wall was the word 'male'. Emma had to walk further around the workhouse until she got to what was little more than a shed to the rear. She went inside and was hit by the deafening silence. Old Montague Street had been bustling with street sellers and horse and carts, barrow boys and ragged children playing with hoops. Here there wasn't the sound of a pin dropping. The smell of rotting flesh invaded her nostrils and she put her handkerchief up to her nose. There were several offices with private scrawled on the doors. She gently tapped on one of them and a man appeared from the room at the end. He was wearing the blue uniform of the workhouse inmates, his hair plastered with grease in a way that made him look like a ventriloquist dummy. Another man stood in the room but didn't come out to greet her.

"Good Afternoon, sir. I've come to see my husband, Joseph Turner. He's had an accident at the sugar refinery."

Emma was careful not to breakdown. Her mother's words echoed in her head. A lady doesn't show emotion.

"Yes mum, he's here. Follow me."

Robert Mann was shocked by the gentile woman. She wasn't the usual inhabitant of Whitechapel. Her tone was that of a gentlewoman. At the end of the offices was a door with 'mortuary' printed in bold lettering. The mortuary assistant opened the door to reveal a small room with a large Belfast sink, a table and, to the side, a wooden gurney with a body that was shrouded with a blood-stained sheet. She held her head up high. Then, with a delicate tug, she exposed the face of her beloved Joseph. Emma quickly put her hand to her mouth. She had never seen a dead body before, and she didn't expect him to be naked. He looked as though he was asleep. There wasn't a mark on his face, yet she could see congealed blood in his hair. She gently touched his cheek and tried with all her might to keep her tears at bay. The assistant placed the sheet back over the body.

"I don't know what I am supposed to do, sir. Can you help me?" He bowed. This woman had manners of the gentry.

"There's a funeral director just on Commercial Street. He does fine funerals and he's trustworthy. The body is looked after if you know what I mean."

"I'm sorry sir. I don't know what you mean."

Robert was keen to help this young woman. She was pleasing to the eye and polite to him and his assistant, James. And that didn't happen very often. He explained that many bodies would be stolen before they were buried and sometimes, after they had been buried, they would be sold to medical students to practice on. Emma held her hand to her mouth. She couldn't believe that anyone would do such a terrible thing. She didn't know that Robert Mann and James Hatfield made a tidy living from the proceeds of supplying bodies to the London Hospital.

"I could assist you and show you the way. Mr Hatfield can stay here and ensure that no one touches your poor dear departed."

Emma nodded. She had to get out of the room as soon as possible. The thought of Joseph being cut up by anyone made her feel violently sick.

The funeral parlour was painted purple with a vase of white lilies in the window. There were two photographs of young children laid out in tiny coffins. Death was never far away in London town, and disease and malnutrition quickly took the very young and the very old. The man behind the counter acknowledged Robert. Emma suspected that there was probably a deal between the two of them. The funeral director was polite, offering numerous services, but Emma told him quickly that she didn't have much money and that they didn't have a family plot.

The bill came to two pounds, three shillings and sixpence. That would include a family plot which could take four people. Emma didn't know where she would get the money from, but it had to be found. She stopped at the pawnbrokers on the way home and sold the silver locket for three shillings.

When she got home, she parcelled Joseph's Sunday jacket and good trousers and took them to the pawnbrokers who gave her another three shillings. It would all go towards the funeral. The rent would be another thing.

Chapter Nine

It was the day of the funeral. Kitty Capstick arrived to help Emma with Arthur. She had a black bonnet covering her red curls.

"Sorry, Mr Capstick is unable to attend the funeral but sends his respects." Work was more important than a neighbour's funeral, money was tight in every household.

"That's all right, Kitty. I understand." Emma was very calm. She looked a very beautiful widow, her hair piled on the top of her head and a black hat perched to the side.

"You seem just like a grand lady. Joseph would have been proud of you my dear."

Emma picked up her gloves and the three went to St Mary's Church on Whitechapel Road. Emma, Kitty, and Arthur sat on one side of the church and Michael and Mary sat on the other. Mary wore a black piece of cloth like a handkerchief, instead of a bonnet. The ceremony was taken by a fat vicar whose red cheeks wobbled as he read the Twenty-Third Psalm. Emma had to smile. She knew that Joseph would have laughed at the scene. As they walked through the graveyard, the rain began, first just a few drops, then a consistent pitter patter. The dampened mourners stood silently as the coffin was lowered into its resting place. Each person passed Emma, taking a handful of earth and throwing it into the dark hole. The earth made musical sounds as it hit the wooden box. Emma said her final farewell and threw her earth softly. Kitty had taken Arthur on home, and Emma thanked Michael and Mary for attending.

"If you want to come back to the house you'd be welcome. I can make tea."

She didn't really want them to come. She wanted to be alone and go to bed and cry, and to smell the sheets that still had the scent of Joe on them.

"I could do with something a bit stronger," said Mary. Michael agreed.

On the way, Michael purchased a bottle of London Gin, and a bottle of porter, at the Ten Bells. Kitty said that he could stay the night and get into bed with her two children Maud and Albert. Emma agreed and went to entertain her unwanted guests. She took a mouthful of the gin. It burned her throat, but she was passed caring. Michael and Mary drank the remainder of the bottle and fell out of the backdoor home.

Emma got undressed and got into bed, her heart was broken. She sobbed and the hot tears soaked into the pillowcase. She fell into a deep fitful sleep, with one nightmare after another. She was woken by Kitty knocking loudly on the back door.

"Arthur wants his mother."

It was ten o'clock. Emma was alarmed at the time. How could she have slept? Arthur was sat on the floor with a saucepan and wooden spoon as Emma prepared herself, washing and brushing her hair. She took her silk purse from the kitchen drawer and counted the money out onto the table. Two pounds, four shillings and sixpence, enough for the funeral. There was just six shillings left. That would pay the rent and for a little food. But then what?

Chapter Ten

Emma didn't want to get into debt. She would have to write to her parents again and tell them of her circumstances. Perhaps she should try to write to one of her brothers. They couldn't turn her away now. Reflecting on her predicament she thought about her Uncle Charles. Perhaps he could be a go-between for her parents and her. She had been his favourite a long time ago. She could only try.

Her uncle lived in a grand terrace of houses at Whitehall. Beautiful carriages with elegant steeds trotted up and down. The ladies wore fine clothes and hats with exotic feathers in them. Emma's memory took her back to the times she had spent at the large house, the fine foods and excitement of London. Kitty willingly took Arthur in, and Emma took the three omnibuses to Whitehall. She departed the smog-filled streets of Whitechapel, to the leafy avenues of Whitehall with its white terraces and polished brass plates. The journey had left her feeling a little sickly. Forty-one, three, five. This was it, forty-five. The lion-head doorknocker gleamed, and she felt its teeth in the palm of her hand. She knocked twice and the sound echoed throughout the house. It was an age, or she thought it was, before a manservant opened one side of the great doors.

"Yes?" He looked at the dusty young woman before him and was about to tell her to remove herself to the back door when she spoke. Emma had pulled herself straight and stood tall.

"I'm here to see my Uncle Charles. Sir Charles Foster. I'm his niece, Victoria Rushworth." She tried to clean her dusty boots on the back of her stockings. The sound of her real name made her feel strange. She had been Emma for so long.

"Ma'am." He wasn't too sure. She looked like a flower seller, but her manners were those of another class. There had been talk of the master's niece running away with one of the servants. This must be the one. He dithered a moment or two, then allowed her to stand in the hallway. The entrance to the house looked to her just the same as it had done years ago, a large gilt mirror gave a reflection she didn't recognise, still a proud young woman, but dressed in dusty clothes wisps of hair dangling down. She licked her fingers and tried to attach them to the mound of hair on top of her head.

"Well, I wondered how long it would be before you darkened my door, young lady. Your mother said you would do so eventually."

Uncle Charles followed the manservant into the hallway. He wore a velvet smoking jacket and a small beret with a tassel that hung to the side.

"Uncle Charles."

She took a step towards him.

"Don't Uncle Charles me, you wicked harlot." He puffed up his chest. Emma could understand why he was hostile. But not as bad as this. She had only fallen in love.

"Please sir, how are my parents? Are they well? And my brothers?" She waited eagerly for the news and welfare of her family.

"Your father is dead and in his grave this past year from a broken heart. Your mother, my dearest sister, in Menston Asylum out of her mind with sorrow. How could you have done it just to have a roll in the hay with a servant?"

Emma looked at the floor. She didn't want to hear anymore.

"So what has happened? Has he left you?"

"My husband is dead. He was killed in an accident. I have a young son, Arthur. He's four years old."

"A bastard then." Emma was shocked at his language and

looked at the floor again. He was right, she and Joseph had not been legally married. The shame was overwhelming her, but she was still proud and lifted her eyes to meet her Uncles.

"Please, Uncle."

"What a pity. You've got what you deserved. Get out and don't come back, or I'll get the servants to throw you into the Thames."

He turned on his heel and let the manservant show her the door. She stood for a moment, unable to move. Her heart was being wrung in a mangle. Her father dead, her husband dead and her mother in Menston Asylum. The servant held his hand out to usher her towards the door. Her feet took the steps, her mind trying to comprehend the tragedy of her life. As she stepped onto the pavement, the door slammed behind her. She walked home sobbing gently, the tears rolling down her face until her eyes were unable to generate more. Emma thought it best to stand on the side of the Thames and throw herself into its putrid waters, washing away her life and her sins. A small animal cry came from a ragged girl, sat on the street. But it wasn't the girl, it was the bundle of rags in the girl's arms, a tiny baby screeching for food. It made her think of Arthur. Someone had to look after him and love him. She couldn't. She wouldn't desert him. She took her handkerchief from her pocket and wiped the tears from her cheeks. Yes, it was Arthur she had to look after now.

Chapter Eleven

When Emma arrived home she had a cry on Kitty's shoulder. But she didn't tell Kitty everything, only that she had found out her father was dead. Kitty gave her a cup of tea with a slug of gin in it to give her solace. She had some news that she thought might be beneficial to Emma. Kitty's husband had told her of a new coffee house opening on Whitechapel Road. They were wanting polite young women to serve. Kitty offered to look after Arthur for sixpence a week. Emma tidied herself up and, after writing down the address, ran the whole way. After a short interview she was taken on for six days a week and every Sunday off. The wages were poor, but she had very little choice. That evening she felt a bit brighter about her future. A knock came to the door and Michael called out her name.

"How are you Emma? How's young Arthur?"

"He's asleep, Michael. He's fine."

She told him about her new job, but needed to get cheaper lodgings, and they had to be close by so Kitty could help with looking after Arthur.

"I know the agent. I'll speak to him tomorrow. There are some cheaper places in the next few streets." He smiled. She looked so vulnerable.

He placed two half crowns on the table. "Here, take this, Emma. It will pay for this week's rent at least."

"I can't, Michael."

He pushed the two coins back to her. "Of course you can."

"Thank you. I'll pay it back." He put his finger to his lips, she smiled at him and thought she was lucky to have Michael as a friend.

***

The next day, Michael had been true to his word and brought the house agent. They went with Emma to look at one room in Dean Street. There was no kitchen range, only a hearth. The privy in the back yard was shared by five other families. The rent was three shillings a week. She'd just be able to afford that, pay Kitty her sixpence, and a few pennies left for food. It was going to be tough, but she was on her own now.

***

Michael and Mary helped Emma and Arthur to move in. Michael had borrowed a hand cart and they managed to get the two armchairs and bed frame complete with horsehair mattress balanced on it. Emma had filled her carpet bag with bedding and Mary carried a box with the pots and pans. They walked through Whitechapel like a family of tinkers. The two rooms smelled of mould and smoke. Emma suspected that the chimney hadn't been cleaned in years.

By nine o'clock in the evening, Emma and Arthur were in the bed with fresh sheets to cover them. Mary had brought fresh bread and a dish of dripping, so their bellies were full. The two slept soundly as the noise of London town bellowed around them.

Chapter Twelve

Emma's life was a series of scenes rushing by. Her new job was interesting. She had never imagined that she would have to work for a living. Women should be at home looking after the children. She wore a uniform that had to be kept clean, a green cotton dress with a white frilled apron over it, and her hair was tied neatly under a white starched bonnet. Part of her duties was to welcome the customers using sir or madam, although there were few women who used the coffee houses. It was a gentleman's habitat, with religion and politics the talking points. The coffee served was thick and black, but Emma loved the smell. It took the stench of tobacco away. She finished most evenings at six o'clock, and she was able to spend a little time with Arthur before he went to bed.

***

One night about eight o'clock there was a knock to the door. It was Michael. He'd been drinking.

"Hello, Milady."

"I'm about to retire. It's very late to call."

"Oh, I just wanted to make sure you were settled."

He pushed the door with his foot and entered. Emma was uneasy. She hated what drink did to men.

"You were happy the other night, and happy to take my money. Now you're too good for us. Mary always said you were a toffee-nosed wench."

"Don't, Michael. I'm grateful for everything you've done for us, but I'm tired."

"How grateful are you?" He leered at her.

"Very grateful of course. I'll pay you back I promise, Michael."

Her voice rose as she sensed he was getting closer to her. She could smell the stale ale and gin on his breath. Her body was pushed backwards towards the kitchen table. He tried to kiss her, first on her lips, then on her throat.

"No, Michael. No. You were Joseph's friend. Don't do this."

Michael tore at her blouse then lifted her onto the table. She didn't scream because Arthur was sleeping in the other room and she didn't want him to witness what was about to happen. He pulled her petticoats up. She struggled, trying to free herself from the strong arms of her attacker.

"Please don't, Michael. I beg you."

"Yes milady, no milady, three bags full milady."

His voice was deep and hoarse as he smothered her body. He took her there on the kitchen table. He was rough, the pain searing through her body. He wasn't a man; he was a wild animal. Thankfully it was over quickly. He rolled off her and fastened his trousers. Emma got up from the table and straightened her petticoats before curling into one of the armchairs. She cried softly.

"Don't cry milady." He laughed again and reached into his waistcoat and put a shilling on the table.

"Here we are. That's the going rate around here."

Michael left, and Emma cleaned herself up. She had been violated by someone she trusted. Emma's anger began to rise, but that subsided when she climbed into the bed next to Arthur. She had to protect them both now.

Chapter Thirteen

Emma's mind wasn't on work, and Mr Barstow had shouted at her for daydreaming. She was serving one of her regular gentlemen when she was jolted back to reality. She apologised to her customer and poured the black steaming liquid into his cup.

She smiled at Mr Drinkwater. "You seem to be far away today my dear."

He was a kind old man, always polite, and always asked to sit where she was serving.

"Tell me what's troubling you."

She didn't tell him her woes. It wouldn't have been right. And Mr Barstow was watching from the main counter. Over the next few weeks Emma couldn't sleep or, if she did, it was with one eye open. She was terrified of Michael returning and what he would do to her. When she went to bed she would tie the door handle to a hook near the mantle. It would give her a little time if Michael tried to force his way in again. In the bedroom she placed a chair under the handle. One Saturday night she was positive she heard it rattle. Her heart was beating out of her chest.

***

On Monday morning at the coffee house Mr Drinkwater took his usual cup.

"Now young Emma, I'd like to ask you something. I do

hope you don't mind."

"No, sir. What can I do for you?"

He shuffled his feet. "You're a well-mannered young woman, someone I could get along with in a business fashion of course. I'm in need of a housekeeper. I understand from Mr Barstow that you are a widow with a small child."

"Yes, sir. Arthur is almost five years old."

"Well the housekeeper will have two bed chambers and a parlour or sitting room. Board is provided of course and a salary of twelve pounds a year, which I think is a fair rate. Well, what do you say?"

Emma couldn't speak at first, it was a dream come true for her. She would be safe from Michael. She would have Arthur to herself and all her worries of paying her rent, and feeding them would disappear. Her eyes told Mr Drinkwater what she had decided. They were two bright stars twinkling back at him.

"That would be wonderful, sir."

"You're too good for this place my dear. I'll expect you by next Friday. Here's the address. Mason, my man, with accommodate you."

The white card he gave her was set out in gold lettering. Mr Archibald Drinkwater M.R.G.S., Willow House, Philpot Street London. Emma felt the excitement rush to her head. She immediately gave notice to Mr Barstow, who was furious about losing one of his best waitresses. She ran home to tell Kitty and Mr Capstick. Kitty's husband, who was the font of all knowledge, said that Mr Drinkwater was well known in the town. He apparently owned business premises and finance buildings across the city. In the excitement that followed, Emma told the couple they could have her beloved armchairs and the bed frame and horsehair mattress. Kitty was thankful, the children were growing, and four-in-a-bed was not the most comfortable of sleeping arrangements. Emma didn't want to take anything from her old life. This was going to be different. She finished her job on Thursday, with Mr Barstow managing to wish her good luck. On Friday with her carpet bag full of odds and ends, she took Arthur and walked hand in hand to Philpot Street. Emma wondered why it was called Willow House there wasn't a tree anywhere. The steps had been scrubbed that morning and the brass numbers on the pillar shone. After knocking and waiting a short time, a manservant opened the front door, Emma presumed that it was Mason. He showed Emma into the morning room, it smelled of tobacco and lavender. The furnishings were velvet and damask, and a roaring fire filled the grate, welcoming the new members of the household.

"The master will be with you shortly." Emma squeezed little Arthur's hand.

She had given her world away for the second time. She hoped third time would be lucky. Mr Drinkwater smiled as he entered the room. He patted his waistcoat.

"Well, well, here we are. My last housekeeper has gone to look after her aged mother in Scotland, so the household is lacking I'm afraid. There's Mason who looks after me, then two or three maids of all work. Mrs Rogers is the cook, and a very fine one too." He slapped his rotund stomach.

"Then there is the pantry boy. Mrs Rogers has the housekeeping books now, but I'm sure she'll be happy to hand them over to you. Mason will show you your quarters. I hope you'll be happy here, and you young Arthur."

Arthur clung to his mother's side. He was frightened of this great house. But he liked the old gentleman.

"My tailor is on Commercial Street. You must go there and get him to make you a couple of dresses suitable for your position here."

"Thank you, sir." She curtsied and followed Mason up the grand staircase.

"There's a back staircase that goes to the kitchen. You'll be expected to use that at other times."

"Of course." She was well aware of the running of a large house and the etiquette between upstairs and downstairs. The bed chambers were on the first floor with a connecting door. The parlour at the end of the corridor was a bright airy room with a large grate that was now burning like a bonfire. At the side of the fireplace was a plate that held a kettle which was singing merrily.

"I told Agnes to prepare tea while you were with the master. I'll allow you to settle into your quarters before I take you down to see the staff."

The room was fitted with comfortable furniture. A walnut table was positioned in the centre, there was a china tea set complete with a milk jug and sugar bowl and silver tongs ready for use. Arthur climbed onto his grand bed which had curtains all the way around. In Emma's chamber the hangings were decorated with red roses, the sheets smelt of lavender. She thought she had died and gone to heaven. She thanked god for bringing her to that place.

Chapter Fourteen

Emma and Arthur settled in the house. It was pure luxury compared to the past five years of scrimping and scraping. Breakfast was brought to Emma every morning at eight o'clock. Arthur was sat on two cushions so he could reach his boiled egg. Luncheon was taken with the staff below stairs. Mr Drinkwater often invited her to take tea with him in the afternoon. He enjoyed her company. She had been educated to a very high standard. He was astonished when he discovered she spoke French. Mr Drinkwater didn't ask of her past, but he knew from her manners and speech she had come from another class. Beneath stairs staff welcomed her, but they also knew she was a step above them. Mrs Rogers was very happy to hand over the accounts and petty cash tin, it had been an extra burden on her. The staff knew Emma as Mrs Turner, only Mason occasionally called her Emma. Her new clothes arrived, and Emma felt a different person. Mrs Rogers gave her the housekeeper's belt, a thick black leather line that held a chain with several keys. There were the front and back doors, the pantry keys, the wine cellar and tanteless key. After breakfast, Mrs Rogers would join her in the parlour. Emma would make a pot of tea and they would discuss the day's menus. Mrs Rogers was impressed at Emma's knowledge of fine foods. Emma would then ensure that the young maids were cleaning correctly and that the pantry boys were not slacking in their duties. The household ran smoothly, and Mr Drinkwater was pleased with his housekeeper.

"Emma, I think young Arthur needs to start his tuition.

He's old enough, and I have someone in mind."

Emma thanked him. It was very generous. What Emma didn't know was that the teacher Mr Drinkwater had in mind was Arnold Coverdale. He had been dismissed from his post at the ragged school because he drank too much and owed Mr Drinkwater for rent. They had come to an agreement to pay the debt by Mr Coverdale giving English and arithmetic lessons to Arthur. The lessons were held in Emma's parlour every morning between ten and twelve. Arthur was soon able to recite rhymes, spell his name and add his numbers. The house became bright and pristine with Emma's care, curtains were cleaned, and carpets brushed. Life settled down and Emma found herself happy in her situation.

"Emma, I'd like you to go to my solicitor on Norfolk Street. I'd normally ask one of the boys to do my errands, but this is most important."

She felt privileged that her master trusted her and agreed, gladly. He handed her the leather file.

"You must hand this to Mr Perkins. No one else."

"Of course, sir."

"Here's the money for the Hackney carriages."

Mason hailed the hackney carriage, which pulled up directly outside the door. She delivered her documents to Mr Perkins and went into the street. The Hackney carriage wasn't there. She looked up and down the busy road. She stepped from the pavement when a carriage and horses bore down onto her. She was frozen to the spot. A large hand reached out and pulled her to safety. The hand belonged to a handsome gentleman of about thirty, with piecing blue eyes.

"Sir, I must thank you. You surely saved my life."

"You're welcome. Patrick Smith esquire at your disposal."

"Mrs Turner." She felt her cheeks flush.

She was certain that he looked a little disappointed. The handsome stranger held a hand up to get a carriage for her. The meeting was over. Emma smiled and sat on the padded seat. It was the first time she had felt that flutter in her stomach after Joseph had passed. Little did she know that this blue-eyed man would feature as a major part of her life.

Chapter Fifteen

It was little over a month after she had taken up residence in Willow House that Emma gave the maid her orders for the day. The room started to go around and she had to sit in a chair to prevent herself from falling over.

"Are you all right, Mrs Turner?" Mary was concerned.

"I'm fine Mary. Go clean the brass on the door."

Emma sat down until she felt better. There had been only one time before when she felt this way. She put her head into her hands. That was the last thing she needed, and how could she have Michael's child when she had been taken in such a violent way? The following day she told Mason that she had errands to run and went to see Kitty. She needed to tell her what had happened with Michael.

"You need some Penny Royal. We can go to the chemist on Brick Lane. You also need a bottle of gin and then put yourself into a hot bath."

Emma wondered how Kitty knew so much. The Penny Royal was sent for, as was a bottle of gin. Emma returned to Willow House. She took a dose of the powder and had young Mary the house maid carry buckets of hot water up to her bed chamber. Emma sat in the almost boiling water and drank half the bottle of gin. After an hour the water was cold, but she had finished the bottle of gin. She was hoping the remedy would work. If it didn't, she would be out on the streets again.

***

It took three days before the powders worked. It was ten days before the bleeding stopped, but she had been saved. Emma had continued working without much disruption, and the household ran like clockwork.

***

Two years had passed quickly at Willow House. Arthur had thrived, and Emma had regained her lost confidence. It was not the life she had been born into, but she was satisfied with her lot. One day Mr Coverdale advised her that he had asked Mary to take young Arthur to his bed chamber. The little boy had complained of stomachache. Emma quickly went to her son's side. He had a fever and complained of pains in his legs. Emma found Mr Drinkwater in his study.

"Please, sir. Arthur is very ill. I'll need to send for a doctor. I'll gladly pay for it out of my salary."

"Don't be foolish, Emma. My doctor will come to tend young Arthur. He'll be fine."

The doctor said that Arthur had just got a chill and, after prescribing pills, said the boy would be better in no time. A large fire was built in the bed chamber and Emma sat by her son's side. She changed the cloth regularly on Arthur's forehead, whispering comforting words to her small son who looked like a little doll in the great bed. She was there two days. On the second day Mr Drinkwater came to visit and check on the patient. He didn't like the colour of the boy, whose pallor was a pale yellow, so the doctor was sent for again. Doctor Brody didn't like the look of the young boy. The doctor shook his head, and he said Arthur had Typhus and there was little else that could be done for him. Emma screamed and hid her head in the bedding.

Arthur slowly slipped from existence. His mother clung to his limp body, her tears drenching the sheets. Mr Drinkwater tore her away and took her to his study. He handed her a large glass of brandy. Mr Drinkwater was visibly upset. He had been fond of the young lad and thought that one day he could be taken on in the firm.

"Emma, I insist on paying for the funeral. He'll have the best send-off. Don't you worry. Young Arthur was like grandson to me."

***

Emma was thankful to her master, but her heart was crushed. She had lost everything. The funeral was held a week later. Arthur was to be interned with his father at St Mary's Church Whitechapel. There was a glass-sided hearse pulled by two fine black stallions which had feathered plumes on their heads. Two small boys dressed in mourning clothes walked slowly before the cortege. Mr Drinkwater had also hired two carriages to follow the hearse, one for himself and Emma, the other for Mason and Mrs Rogers. Kitty and George were waiting at the church with Maude and Albert. The tiny coffin was lowered into the earth, and Emma was unable to refrain from sobbing out loud.

***

Back at Willow House Mr Drinkwater gave Emma a glass of his best brandy. The cure for all ails.

"You need a day or two rest, Emma. I insist. Mrs Rogers can take over your duties."

Emma thanked him and retired to her bed chamber. A little while later she put on her shawl and told Mrs Rogers she was going for a walk. She needed the fresh air. She walked to Hope Street and knocked at Kitty's door. She was Emma's only friend and she needed her. Kitty led her to the armchair and made a cup of tea. They both cried and laughed in sequence as they reminisced about the birth and early years of Arthur. George Capstick had bought a bottle of gin and they shared the liquor. Emma walked home alone, although Kitty advised it wasn't safe. Emma didn't care, she didn't want to live anymore. She didn't have anyone. They had been ripped from her. God had been cruel. She was paying for her sins once again.

***

Mr Drinkwater invited Emma to tea a week after Arthur's funeral.

"It's time to return to your duties Emma. It isn't fair on the other staff. I realise it is a difficult time, but we need you."

He was being kind. She thanked him for being patient and said she would be back the next day.

***

As she ensured the fires had been made correctly in the morning, she went to the master's study. The fire was roaring and the smell of the Turkish tobacco hung in the air. She checked the contents of the decanters. The honey coloured liquid inside looked appealing. She took her key and opened the Tantalus. With a shaking hand she poured a herself a glass of brandy. She took a large gulp and her body thanked her for the pleasure, as the fluid ran through her veins and awoke her tired limbs. She went to the kitchen and washed the glass, returning it to the study. Mason was already there.

"Mrs Turner, Emma, you must stop this. I have a duty to report the theft of the master's liquor. He has been a fair and generous employer. If it happens again, I'll report it."

Emma's eyes dropped to the floor and her face reddened. She said she was sorry and that it wouldn't happen again.

"Mrs Rogers keeps the sherry below stairs. If you need a bottle in your parlour she will provide you with one. But being drunk on duty is a dismissible offense."

Emma didn't tell Mason she already had a bottle of sherry in her parlour, but the brandy was so much stronger. A glass would make her feel able to function. It would take a whole bottle of sherry to get the same effect.

***

On two or three mornings that week, Mason was summoned by Mrs Rogers. Emma had not gotten up, and he had to go to her bed chamber and shake her until she woke. The master had asked to see the accounts and Emma had not prepared them.

"I am so sorry, sir," she said as she finally sat before him.

"This will not do, Mrs Turner. I'm a busy man. I can't be waiting on you. What's your excuse?"

"I have none, sir. I overslept this morning. I'm very sorry."

"Overslept? Hen's teeth. I don't employ servants who oversleep and lay in their beds."

Mr Drinkwater was very angry. He puffed on his clay pipe and picked up the account books. Luckily the accounts were in order and, after an hour, Emma was given leave. She would have to curb her appetite for the drink, but it was the only thing that could blot out the loss of Joseph and Arthur. Emma had the pantry boy go to the pot shop and buy gin for the staff. The master allowed a ration of one glass every day, as well as one glass of porter She added a couple of extra bottles for herself. Almost every day, Emma would have a glass of Sherry before her breakfast tea and a dash in the tea itself. Mason had noticed she was not always steady on her feet. On one occasion Emma fell down the back stairs. Mrs Rogers had a word with Mason who thought he had no alternative but to tell the master. Emma was summoned to the study,

"You have disappointed me Mrs Turner," said Mr Drinkwater. "I gave you a home here at Willow House and I thought I had chosen wisely. You've made a fool of me. We could have had a long working relationship, but I won't have theft. I like to think that I'm a generous man and that I treat my staff well. But I am the master in my home, and I don't employ drunkards and thieves. You are dismissed, and you will leave by the end of the week. I owe you six shillings which is far more than you deserve, and I will not give you a reference."

He didn't say anymore, but got up from the desk and left the room. Emma was dumbstruck. He was a good master. She had taken advantage of his generosity. She had acted in such a bad way. Now she felt foolish. She dealt with it the only way she knew how, by finishing the bottle of sherry in her parlour. Emma tried to speak to Mr Drinkwater on several occasions, but he held his hand up in front of him and called for Mason. She hadn't realised that he didn't really want to dismiss her, but he had to keep the respect of the other members of staff. On Friday Mason helped her into a hackney carriage with her few belongings including the jet necklace with locket Mr Drinkwater had given to her that held a lock of Arthur's hair, and her Sunday dress and underskirts. Her whole life was in one bag. The carriage took her to the only place she knew, Hope Street.

Chapter Sixteen

Kitty welcomed the tearful Emma. She made tea.

"You poor dear. After all you've been through, you can stay here until you get yourself sorted. We can push the two chairs together."

Emma handed two shillings to Kitty to go towards her board.

"Well that's a treat. We'll have some fine morsels tonight."

In the evening after a good meal of dumplings and carrots, George Capstick suggested that the two women join him at the Ten Bells for a glass of ale. Emma was pleased. She had found a longing for the alcohol to numb her brain, which was racing. All she could see when she closed her eyes was Arthur laid in his sick bed, or Joseph on the wooden gurney in the mortuary. The three sat by the fire in the tavern. It was a busy night but fuel was expensive, so it was better to warm your hands on the inns coal fire than burn your own coal. There was a small cloud that hung just above them from the tobacco that was blown out from the clay pipes. Most of the men, and a few of the women, smoked. Emma felt sorry for her fellow drinkers. They had few choices in their lives, but she had chosen hers. She felt different from the others in her company although she was closer to them now than she had ever been.

As Emma gulped the gin, and as it swept through her body, the voices and pictures in her head began to disappear. She laughed at George's jokes and she watched the others that were at the bar. She was a little afraid that Michael would suddenly appear. What she did notice was a pair of fine blue eyes. The creases at the corner of the eyes turned upwards. The handsome stranger headed straight for their table. She got a little closer to Kitty.

"It's him Kitty," Emma whispered.

"Mrs Turner, you're not the person I thought I would meet tonight."

"Sir." Emma nodded.

"And, please, introduce me to your husband." He held his hand out to George who looked confused.

"No, sir, you are mistaken. These are my friends, Mr and Mrs Capstick. I'm a widow."

Patrick asked if he could join them at the table. He had good manners. He bought a bottle of rum and the group enjoyed each other's company. Emma was in a whirl. This man was about to whisk her off her feet.

Chapter Seventeen

In less than a month of meeting at the tavern, Emma was in love again. It wasn't the love she had with Joseph, but, rather, the need to get close to someone, to share a bed, to feel the touch of another human being.

***

They walked in the park one Sunday. The bandstand had a dozen musicians playing loudly. The couple sat on a wooden bench and listened, their feet tapping to the beat of a popular tune. Patrick felt into his waistcoat pocket and pulled out a small velvet box.

"This is for you, Emma. We can get married if you wish to. I would like you to be mine, Mrs Smith."

Emma looked at the tiny gold band. She took it out and put it on the third finger of her left hand.

"I will, Patrick."

He jumped up and shouted with joy.

"Come, we need to celebrate."

They went to the nearest gin shop and drank to each other's health.

"I only have one room. I never needed much more. Its nothing fancy."

She didn't care. She was sleeping on a chair now. It had to be one up from that. They went back to the Capsticks. Patrick said he would come for her at midday the next day.

"Are you sure you'll be all right, Emma? George has heard some bad things about Patrick."

"What things? Look, Kitty, he's bought me a ring." She held up her hand and the gold band twinkled.

"Where does he get his money from?" Kitty asked, her hands on her hips.

"His work is carrying out deliveries and he buys and sells goods. You know he's kissed the blarney stone."

Emma wasn't happy to be questioned by Kitty. The older woman was quite glad that Emma was going. It had been okay for a couple of weeks, but it was a little crowded in the two of rooms. George was also pleased Emma was to be away. It was getting more and more difficult to find the money to feed them all. Patrick was true to his word. He arrived at midday and helped Emma to carry the carpet bag and her other bits. They reached Dorset Street. The house was a grey three-storey building. Every window was dirty with cobwebs draped down like brocade curtains. Patrick opened the door to his room and Emma's heart fell. There was a strong smell of stale body odour and dead mice. There was a trundle bed in the corner, a kitchen range, a small wooden table and two three legged stools. The mantle was littered with empty gin and porter bottles. The table had a jug of sour beer and half a loaf of mouldy bread.

"I know it doesn't look much, Emma, but with a woman's touch it'll be fine."

Emma thought it wasn't a woman's touch, but a small miracle needed to change the room. She sent Patrick out to buy sheets for the bed and two feather pillows with cases. He had told her that he had a few shillings to tidy the place up and Emma refused to get into a bed without sheets. He went off with a list of household items that she needed. Emma boiled water on the range and began scrubbing the floor. When Patrick eventually returned, he thought he had walked into the wrong room. The range was lit and had been black-leaded, the floor smelled fresh, the table scrubbed with a cloth placed on it complete with a posy of violets in a jar. Emma had made the bed with the new sheets, too. She was at last satisfied to be there.

"Well, Mrs Smith, I'm taking you out to eat. The Britannia Tavern is serving steak and oyster pie and I think you deserve it."

Emma agreed. They had a riotous evening, eating, drinking and laughing. When they returned to Dorset Street, they couldn't keep their hands of each other, tumbling into the fresh bed, making love intensely.

When Emma awoke next day, Patrick wasn't there. She had presumed he had gone to work. She washed and drank a small glass of gin. There wasn't any tea in the house and her throat was dry.

Patrick arrived home eager to make love to Emma again. The man had an appetite for her, drinking in her smell and tasting every part of her body.

"Come on my girl. You're too beautiful to be sat in this room. I want the world to see what a lucky man I am."

She dressed carefully, pulling her hair up into two combs that Patrick had bought her.

"Just look at you. The lady of Whitechapel."

She blushed as he placed her hand into the crook of his arm. They ate potted shrimps and apple dumplings, and a bottle of rum finished the evening off well.

"Tell me about your work, Patrick."

"I do all sorts, deliveries for people that pays well sometimes. I also look after a friend's barrow at Spitalfields market. You don't have to worry, I always have something on. The money's always coming in."

She smiled at him. He had a secret the same as herself, so she didn't press anymore. Emma knew he had arrived from Ireland fifteen years ago to make his fortune. What she didn't know was in Ireland he had been beaten by his father, almost every day since being a young lad. When Patrick was fourteen, his father had come home from the pub and started to take his belt off to give him yet another beating. He was unsteady on his feet so Patrick took his opportunity and jumped up with the flat iron and caved his father's head in. When his father fell to the floor, his mother screaming at his side. He hit him again until there was blood and brains on the rag rug. His mother tried to stop the bleeding with her apron, but she needn't have bothered. Her husband was dead. Patrick watched his mother nursing her husband's body and thought how strange it was that she had never comforted him, when his father had beaten him until his body was covered in blood. Patrick went through his father's pockets and found two shillings. He said goodbye to his mother and ran across the fields. Patrick asked for a lift from a farmer who was going to the ferry with cheeses, and was told to climb aboard. The ferry men were loading to try and catch the next tide. Patrick managed to sneak into the hold. He wasn't sure where the boat was going, but the cheese was bound for England and that would be far enough away from the murder he had just left.

He awoke to shouting and movement in the hold. Carefully he slipped away from his hiding place and put his feet on dry land. He was at the port of Liverpool and had never seen so many people all rushing and pushing, doing whatever they had to do. Liverpool wasn't the place he wanted to be. He wanted to go to London where the streets were paved with gold. He'd heard many stories of young men like himself who had made their fortune there.

He was a strong boy. In Ireland he had been expected to start work on a farm, something he wasn't too interested in doing. Patrick was a capable lad with the savvy to make his own way in the world. He worked, he stole, he begged, until he reached London. He met a few boys or young men like himself who were without lodgings or jobs. They got together to help each other. Whitechapel was the cheapest place in London to live so they shared a room for a few coppers, and slept on the bare floorboards. It was better than the cold hard pavement. When one of them got a little work they all ate or they would steal food to avoid starvation. Patrick was lucky enough to get a job with an accountant. He had always been good with numbers so had no trouble completing the test that was set for him. His employer was an old Jew, Mr Sachs, who didn't have a problem with Patrick being Irish or Catholic. He had also suffered discrimination so was glad to give him the post. With a regular income, Patrick was able to take lodgings at Mrs Owen's on Flower Street. He shared his room with another young clerk, Robert. Mrs Owen provided tea, bread and dripping for breakfast and, on an evening, there was some sort of broth with bread or on Saturdays, a bloater.

Patrick thought his life was good and could see himself doing well in the firm. It was when Mr Sachs asked him to go to the city bank there was a problem. He gave Patrick four pounds and six shillings to be deposited. Patrick could feel the money burning in his pocket. He'd never felt so much. He stopped off at the tavern near the bank and drank a glass of beer.

His mother's voice was in his ear. "Patrick, don't take the money. It's not yours."

The devil spoke in his other ear. "Take it, take it. Why would you not? You could live like a king."

The devil won. He collected his armful of belongings from Mrs Owens and moved nearer to the Thames. Within a month he had spent it all, and was living on the streets again. He didn't regret his folly, he enjoyed the excitement while it lasted. Then, that first time he met Emma, he'd fallen in love. She was a lady, someone he thought would never look at him but, when their eyes met, he knew she had the same feeling. And now they were living as man and wife. She wore his ring. Patrick enjoyed the domesticated life. He liked the way that Emma looked after him. She was a good cook and very careful with the housekeeping. The room was clean most of the time, it was just when they had drunk too much the previous night that Emma took a long time to rise. Patrick had never known a woman who could down a bottle of gin and still walk in a straight line. They had begun drinking most nights in the local hostelry and were well known by the landlords.

***

Emma was getting dressed one morning. She tried to fasten the button on the side of her skirt, but the material wouldn't meet. She felt the roundness of her stomach. Pregnant. She hadn't had the usual sickness. Patrick wasn't as excited as Joseph had been. Children weren't a feature he'd expected to feature in his life. His mother had given birth to thirteen, and he was the only one still alive. Most of his brothers and sisters hadn't reached the age of five before they were laid to rest. Maybe that was the reason his father had beaten him so much. He was a survivor.

When Emma's time came she sent Patrick for Kitty, her guardian angel. It happened within two hours. A tiny grey girl appeared, looking more like a skinned rabbit which might have hung in the market, than a baby. Kitty wrapped the package tight and handed her to Emma. Kitty shook her head and Patrick slammed the door on the way to the tavern.

"I'm sorry, Emma. She's a very sickly child."

Kitty stroked Emma's forehead.

"She'll be all right, Kitty. Why would you say that?"

Emma looked at the child.

"She has all her limbs, fingers and toes. Yes, she's small, but she'll grow."

"I can smell her. She smells sweet. That's a bad sign."

Emma sniffed at the baby. There was a sweet smell but nothing offensive. The child let out a short scream, then took its last breath. Emma held her close and cried. She had wanted another child to care for, someone to replace Arthur. The tea Kitty made was laced with gin. Emma drank and fell back onto her pillow and went to sleep.

***

Later that evening Patrick returned.

"I'm sorry. She was so weak."

"That's what happens. It's the way of the world." He was so cold.

"We need to bury her, Patrick. Where can we get the money from? I want her to be with Arthur. Brother and sister together."

"Don't be stupid woman. We don't have two pennies to rub together. Where are we going to get two or three pounds? They won't bury her in the graveyard. She hasn't been christened."

"She has to be buried, Patrick. You can't just throw our daughter away like a piece of rubbish." Patrick sat and thought awhile, puffing on his clay pipe.

"Come, get out of your bed."

Emma dressed as Patrick covered the tiny body in sheeting, then lay it in a coal sack along with the shovel from the kitchen range.

"What are you doing?"

He didn't answer her but took her arm.

"It's St Marys Church where Arthur is, isn't it?"

"Yes," she answered. They headed for the churchyard. It was quite dark and eerie as they made their way through gravestones. Emma could still hear the hawkers on Whitechapel Road. The stillness of the night gave her chills and the hoot of an owl made her get closer to Patrick. They passed giant crosses and marble mausoleums. By the ash tree was a small wooden cross. Joseph's name was printed with the date of death. Underneath was Arthur's birth date and death. Patrick dug down about eighteen inches and put the swaddled infant into the hole, then covered her with damp earth.

"You can come back another day with a pencil and add her to the cross."

"What shall we name her, Patrick?"

"Clara. It's a fine name."

He felt a lump in his throat. He did have a heart after all. Patrick thought all feeling had left him over the years. Emma said a short prayer. She had understood why Patrick had done this. She didn't want Clara to be buried in a paupers' grave. She should be with her brother.

They both walked back, arm in arm, stopping at the pot shop to buy a bottle of gin.

***

Emma would visit the graveyard every Sunday, taking a bunch of violets or daisies with her. The small wooden cross now had Clara's name etched under Arthur Turner. Patrick didn't go with her. He never thought of Clara again. He was only interested in the living.

Chapter Eighteen

Emma's life didn't seem to change. She and Patrick would frequent the taverns and inns in the area. One Saturday night they found themselves at the far end of Dorset Street. The Britannia was full of sailors on shore-leave having a merry time. The piano in the bar was silent, but now and again someone would try to get a tune out of it. Emma, having had two or three glasses of gin, went over and started to play a popular melody. Patrick was amazed, a crowd thronged around her and sang to the tune with all joining in to sing the chorus. When she'd finished, they begged her to play again but she refused. She could see Patrick in the corner of the inn and he wasn't happy. As they left the tavern, the landlord shouted at her to return again soon.

"You didn't tell me you could play the piano."

"You didn't ask."

She knew she should not have answered him. A fist appeared before her and smashed into her mouth. The blood spurted out along with one of her teeth. People passed, but no-one intervened. Two soldiers laughed as Patrick kicked her as she lay curled into a ball on the ground. Emma didn't cry. She was too shocked, the blood spilling across the pavement and running into a small pool.

"How dare you make a spectacle of yourself when you were out with me. Remember you're my wife, and I will tell you if you play for people. Do you understand I'm here to look after you?"

From then on Emma guarded her tongue. She didn't want to lose any more teeth. She tried to smile without showing the gap. This was a time she could have used a fan. Patrick sometimes suggested she played when he thought they were in an establishment where they would be given free drinks, but he didn't like the attention Emma got. She noticed that he didn't really need an excuse to hit her, pull her hair or kick out at her, he seemed to like the power he had over her. Regular beatings made her want to leave but where could she go? Kitty had her own problems with Maude having a baby. There wasn't any room for Emma. She tried to keep Patrick as sweet as possible, but it was difficult. He would often tell Emma as he left for work to meet him at a particular tavern at around six o'clock. They would eat and drink until it was late. On one such occasion Emma coiled her hair under her bonnet and went to meet Patrick at The Three Compasses. When she got through the door, she saw Patrick sweet-talking a girl of sixteen or so at the bar, his arm around her waist.

The young girl laughed. Patrick was already drunk. "Oops. Here comes the wife."

"Just waiting for you, my sweet."

They sat in the corner and drank the night away. Next morning Patrick didn't say anything about his dallying, but Emma couldn't hide her sadness.

"We can meet up tonight and go to the Music Hall as a treat. How about that?"

"Yes Patrick. But will you be alone?" He laughed.

"Don't be jealous my sweet. It doesn't become you." He left to do some deliveries.

In the late afternoon, Emma dressed and put a little rouge on her cheeks. She walked to the inn and Patrick was waiting. Emma was relieved that he was alone. Later they took in a performance at the music hall and ate baked potatoes for supper. The taverns were busy, and Patrick and Emma joined in the merriment. After relieving herself in the backyard privy, Emma returned to find that Patrick had been joined by two sailors, a bottle of rum and four glasses on their table.

"Look at this my sweet. I've got two friends here that want to share their grog."

Emma smiled trying not to show the gap in her teeth. The rum was strong and worked a treat. They sang sea shanties and told jokes.

"I've told Michael, and, is it, John?" Patrick pointed at the sailor that had long whiskers.

"Yes. I told Michael and John that you would give them a little kiss for being so generous with their liquor." Emma was mortified.

"No Patrick. I can't do that."

"Yes you can. I said you would. You wouldn't want me to lie to them, would you?" Emma recognised the glint in the icy blue eyes.

"Just a little kiss."

The two sailors laughed and each took turns to take Emma into their arms and plant wet kisses upon her lips. She wiped her mouth with the back of her hand. How could Patrick do such a thing? The four finished the bottle and another was ordered. Emma started to feel uncomfortable. She had to refuse a couple of drinks just so she was aware what was going on. The customers in the tavern sang together, and everyone had a good time, all apart from Emma. She sat quietly in the corner awaiting her fate. The embers were dying down in the grate, and the landlord said it was time for his bed. He collected bottles and glasses from the tables.

"Now Emma, thank these brave young men, and properly mind."

Emma stood up and curtsied saying thank you. The sailors laughed and pushed each other.

"I said properly my girl." Patrick shouted.

The two sailors approached her and kissed her soundly on the lips. She showed her disgust by wiping the saliva from her face. They all walked outside.

"That's rude, Emma. These nice boys deserve better manners. You've drunk their grog all night. They could have had a tuppenny harlot sat on their knees."

The two men agreed with Patrick. Emma walked in front

of the three men just wanting to get home. The drink had made her a little unsteady on her feet, so she held onto the wall now and again. They reached the corner of Dorset Street. Patrick caught up with her.

"Do what I say woman." He put his arm around her neck.

"Please don't hurt me, Patrick," Emma begged.

"I'm not going to hurt you. But I will if you don't shut up."

"Here you are lads. Get a feel of a real lady here, free with her wares."

The two sailors laughed and surrounded Emma. Patrick held her neck while the men felt every part of her body. With their rough hands they squeezed her breasts, and one had his hand under her skirts. She couldn't struggle as Patrick had her in a hold so tight she could barely breathe. The taller of the soldiers dropped the front of his trousers, Emma jerked away but Patrick held on with a steel like grip.

"No lads, that would be an extra two shillings at least."

"No, Patrick. Please." Emma begged him again.

The lad fastened up his trousers, he could have a willing partner for two pennies.

"Come on, Michael. Let's be off." The sailors stumbled away in the dark night to find a much more agreeable woman.

Patrick was furious. He hit Emma in the stomach with his fist then, as she lay on the floor, kicked her two or three times. He left her to crawl home alone.

***

He was in bed when she eventually got back. Emma tried to get into bed, but Patrick kicked her out. She pulled the trundle out at the foot of the bed then used her shawl as a pillow and fell asleep. When she awoke, Patrick was still in bed. She crept in at the side of him, first kissing his shoulder and his back. Patrick turned around and they enjoyed a moment of pleasure. As they dressed, Emma spoke softly.

"Patrick, you can't give me away. I'm your wife, if in

name only."

"There you are again, complaining those two lads only wanted a bit of fun. They had let us share their liquor all night. It hadn't cost us a penny. You're never grateful, Emma. Never." She stared at the floor, frightened to look into his eyes.

"I have some business in town. You can come too. The Britannia about six and make yourself look presentable."

After he had gone, she looked at herself in the mirror. She was a mess. The drink had taken its toll, her hair no longer had a shine, and the lack of good food made her skin take on a yellow pallor. She was a bag of bones, her clothes hanging from her thin frame. She took a cup of tea and gin, her usual breakfast. Emma opened the small wooden box from under the bed. It was the locket that held Arthur's curl of hair. She gently kissed the locket before returning it to its box. How had she sunk so low? She wallowed in self-pity for most of the afternoon. She had lost the love for life and had no pride in herself or for her home. She barely had the effort to put one foot in front of the other. At six o'clock, she walked the short distance to the Britannia. Patrick was stood, again, with the horse-faced young woman. Emma nodded in acknowledgement and sat at a table. Patrick joined her five minutes later with two glasses of ruby red port.

"Now my dear, I need to talk to you. Money is very tight, and you need to be pulling your weight. We're both fond of the bottle. You won't be free with your wares but there's something you can do."

Emma shook her head. She could keep her dignity and make sure they had money for living.

They went into a tavern they didn't often frequent. They had a couple of gins for courage. Patrick stood at the bar as Emma nervously sat at a table near the fire. An elderly gent sat across from her. He drank his beer and passed the time of day with Emma. When he heard her speak, he looked at her again.

"I do not think you are from these parts madam."

"No, sir. I'm from the north, visiting my aunt on Thrawl

Street."

"Oh yes, I know it well." He finished his ale and checked his pocket watch. "Must be off. Good evening, Madam."

"I'm on my way also. May I walk part of the way with you?"

He wasn't sure, but she did speak so well.

"No problem."

They set off together, Patrick a little way behind. They got to part of the street where the gas light was low. Patrick was quick and knocked the old man to the ground, snatching his pocket watch and emptying his pockets. Emma screamed and ran as fast as her bony legs would carry her back home.

***

Ten minutes later Patrick came in and placed the fob watch and ten shillings on the table.

"You did well gal." Emma was upset. She wanted to know if the old man was all right.

"He was fine, shouting for help down the street"

"He was just an old man, Patrick. How could you hurt him?"

"I only knocked him down. He deserved it, chatting up my missus."

Emma was disgusted with herself. She was now a thief, whoring would be next. Emma prayed that Patrick had a job the next day. She couldn't go through that again.

***

Patrick was up and off, thankfully God had heard her. He had left her a shilling, so she took the jug up to the pot shop and bought a pint of gin and a dish of chicken stew. She wouldn't have to meet Patrick, therefore wouldn't have to drag another unsuspecting gentleman to their demise.

***

Patrick arrived home at eight o'clock. He was furious she had not been to the Britannia and gave her a good thrashing, just so she would remember. Emma took her beating. She was too drunk. She hardly felt it, and she didn't care.

"You had better be at the tavern tomorrow gal. Six o'clock. Don't forget."

***

The threat was enough. He didn't leave any money and, by five o'clock, she had a terrible thirst. She applied a little rouge and put her bonnet on.

Patrick was already in the pub with his young dalliance. Emma sat near the fire until Patrick joined her. He set a jug of ale down in front of her and the way that he spoke made her believe that he had been there all day. He called Emma terrible names; the girl smirked as Emma's face turned red with embarrassment. Two men joined them at the table. Patrick obviously knew them, and they greeted Emma, who spoke to them politely.

"You were right, Paddy. She's a toff. What are you doing with her you scoundrel?"

They all laughed together. It was a good-humoured evening with gin and ale flowing freely. The men were in deep discussion, whispering between themselves, plotting something illegal, Emma thought. But the fire was warm, and the gin was making her dizzy. She didn't care a fig what they were planning to do. When they arrived home, Patrick didn't get into bed. Instead he paced the floor. Emma could feel something was about to happen. Any slight noise made him jump. He had his leather cosh in his hand as though waiting for someone to attack him.

"Tell me what's happening, Patrick. You're frightening me."

She tried to calm him down. Eventually he joined her in the bed holding her tight.

"I'm sorry. I haven't been good to you, Emma. But this job will see us with money. We can move away from here, go to the country or to the sea."

Emma thought the sea would be nice, but she didn't like the idea of what Patrick was going to have to do to get there. In the evening, instead of going to the tavern, Patrick bought a jug of ale and a bottle of gin. He gave Emma a shilling.

"I may not be back in the morning, so this money will get you some food. You can make me something nice for my supper."

"Patrick, I'm frightened."

"Don't be silly gal. I'll be fine. It's something I have to do."

At midnight, Patrick put on his jacket and wrapped his scarf around his face, only his eyes peeping over the top. He quietly shut the door behind him. Emma drew back the corner of the curtain. She saw Patrick meet the two men from the tavern. They slapped each other on the backs as though they were great friends. She felt completely out of her depth. How had she sunk so low? In her other life she could have been at the Opera, or entertaining the elite in a grand house in Yorkshire or on a gondola in Venice. But then she wouldn't have had Joseph's love or her darling boy, Arthur. She didn't count Patrick as a love. He was just a necessity, just a part of life. She didn't think that Patrick loved her. She didn't think he loved anyone. He had been hurt in his past life that prevented him from loving.

Chapter Nineteen

Emma had drunk most of the gin, and half of the jug of ale, she passed out on the bed fully clothed. The sun shone through a chink in the curtains making Emma blink awake. She had a terrible headache but that wasn't unusual. After tea and gin, she washed her face and decided to go to the market for Patrick's supper. She bought mutton and vegetables to make a stew with some pearl barley. The stew bubbled gently on the fire most of the day. At six o'clock in the evening Patrick had not returned, a couple of hours later still no sign of him. Emma had bought half a pint of gin and consumed it while she waited. She sat at the kitchen table all night hoping Patrick would just walk through the door. Next day Emma went to the Britannia Inn, she asked Patrick's acquaintances if they had seen her husband, they all shook their heads. She walked further onto the Ten Bells Tavern and asked the landlord who pointed to an old man in the corner.

"Ask Archie, he knows everything." Archie had great side whiskers and a handlebar moustache.

"Sir, I am asking about my husband, Patrick Smith he hasn't come home, I was told you might know where he is?" The old man looked around the room to check if anyone was listening.

"Oh, Paddy Smith I knows him, I think he has been up to no good, the peelers have got him and one of his mates Charlie Peace down at Whitechapel goal."

Emma sat on the stool at the side of Archie, she wanted to

put her head on his shoulder and cry. Her face was that of someone who had given up on life.

"Steady girl, have a drink with old Archie you can't do anything for him now."

Emma refused the offer, then decided it might be the last drink she had for a while.

"I'll just have a small one, you are very generous sir." The old man thought Paddy's wife had a lovely manner about her and tried to get her to stay a while longer.

"No, I need to return home."

She slung the last drops of gin to the back of her throat. Emma was hoping that Patrick would be waiting for her, but he wasn't, she went to Kitty's.

"Come on in Emma, what's wrong my dear you look terrible, come and see what we have?" Emma walked into the room where Maud was sat with her new baby, a girl with red golden curls.

"Oh, Maud when did this happen?"

"Last night." Maud gave a weak smile.

"She's beautiful what are you to call her?" Maud proudly proclaimed, "Emma after you."

Emma took the baby from her and cuddled the poor mite. She felt very guilty, but Maud didn't know any different.

"I'm proud of you naming her after me. Thank you." She gave the baby back to twelve-year-old Maud, who was little more than a baby herself.

"Can I talk to you Kitty?" She needed some privacy.

Kitty took her into the bedroom. Emma wondered how on earth Kitty, George, Albert, Maud and the baby would all fit into the two rooms. She noticed that the bottom drawer from the tall boy had been made into a cot for the baby but that wouldn't last for long.

"What's ailing you Emma, you don't look as though you have slept?"

Emma said she hadn't. She told Kitty of what had happened to Patrick.

"He has been locked up, but I don't know where he is or what will happen to him. I have no money the landlord will be coming on Friday and I'm already a week behind."

She felt that there was too much for her to handle, she had her head in her hands.

"I'm sorry Kitty, you have enough of your own problems to deal with, but you are the only person I have left in the world."

"That's all right my love, George will be home in a moment he will know what to do."

Kitty made tea and Emma had another cuddle of the baby.

"Young Albert has got a job as an errand boy at the stock yard it's all extra and we need it with another mouth to feed."

George was home a moment later, he wasn't keen on Emma being there she was trouble he thought, trouble with a begging bowl. Kitty relayed what had happened, but George already knew about it. It was common knowledge that one of the Wharfe offices were burgled by three men. They attacked the two night-watchmen, and one of them was in a serious way. However, two of the men had been caught red handed, with the cash tin and two barrels of brandy. They had been up before the beak yesterday but would be in court next Wednesday because it was serious. Emma cried not for Patrick he was a fool, but for herself. She was alone again, with no opportunity to get herself out of the mire. Emma had her miracle with Mr Drinkwater, and she had thrown that away, she was at the very bottom of humanity. George said the times of the assizes were posted on the board outside the court. She took herself up to the city and found the court, there was a list of the court sessions for the following week. Emma quickly went through the names, until she reached the right one. The crown against Patrick (Paddy)Smith nine thirty a.m. court one.

Chapter Twenty

Emma had been struggling to feed herself. She only had one decent thing to sell, the jet locket with Arthur's piece of hair. Emma took the hair out and pressed it with some paper before putting it inside a pocket of her petticoat. The pawnbroker gave her a shilling. It was worth more, but she didn't have the heart to barter for another half penny. She bought bread and a heel of cheese and, to wash it down, a jug of ale. As she ate her feast, there was a knock to the door.

"Landlord here, Mr Smith. Landlord." Emma went to the door.

"My husband is away on business, sir."

The landlord smirked. "Do you think I'm stupid missus? Paddy Smith is in the goal and will be there for a very long time to my guessing."

Emma dropped her head. "Please give me another week, sir. I'll try to get the money together."

She didn't know why she was offering. She would never be able to pay the rent or the three weeks that they already owed.

"I'll tell you what's going to happen Mrs Smith. I want you out by Friday, do you hear? And I'll be bringing my boys around to make sure you go."

Emma understood the threat. She went through the room looking for things to sell. There was a jacket of Patrick's and the sheets on the bed. If she was to be on the streets she may as well take them to the pawn shop. Four pennies sat on the counter, all that was between Emma and the street. She didn't know what she could do.

***

She thought of going to the workhouse, but she had to have a drink, her throat was dry and she needed to drown her sorrows. She went to the Britannia. The horse faced girl came up to her.

"I've heard about poor Patrick. Do you think he'll be sent down?"

"I don't know." Emma poured the bottle of gin slowly into the glass not wanting to spill a drop.

"I'm Kate by the way." She plonked herself onto the seat at the side of Emma.

"Hello Kate. I don't really want a conversation at the moment."

"I understand. I've been in the same position and I think you need a friend right now."

Kate pushed her empty glass towards the bottle of gin.

"Not friends who have a thirst like mine." Emma poured half a glass of the liquid into Kate's glass.

"I live in a room near here. I can put you up for a few days. You'll have to sleep on the bottom of the bed or, if I have company, you'll have to make yourself scarce."

"That's very kind of you Kate but you don't know me."

"I know enough." She smiled at Emma.

"I have to be out of my lodgings by Friday. I've no work, no money."

"Then come on Thursday. Twelve o'clock."

"Thank you, Kate. I'm going to the assizes on Wednesday to see Patrick."

"Do you want me to come with you?"

"No, I want to do this alone."

The two drank the bottle of gin, and Emma thanked her and stumbled home. When she opened the door of the room she took in the scene. Before her was a dirty hovel, the grate was full of ash, void of a shovel of coal to warm her freezing hands. The floor was dirty and dusty, not swept for weeks. And now she was having to move again.

***

At nine in the morning the doors to the assizes opened and a lanky policeman shoved the mob who wanted to get into the public gallery like pigs in a pen. Emma sat on a bench close to the jury stalls.

"No eating or drinking in the public gallery. Quiet in the court," the usher shouted from the front.

The door from the cells opened and Patrick and Charlie climbed the steps to the defendant's box. Emma gave a small wave to Patrick who looked as though he hadn't slept. His hair was matted, and his usual clean-shaven face now had a scruffy beard. Patrick didn't wave back. He just looked at the floor. The woman behind her shouted out to the other man.

"Charlie my love, we're here for you."

The policeman who had stood at the doorway walked over to the public gallery and told her to be quiet.

"Silence in the court. Be up-standing for the Honourable Judge Charles Lawton."

Everyone stood until the Judge had taken his place, the usher then motioned for them to sit. The case was read out, the prosecution said there was no defence, the culprits Patrick (Paddy) Smith and Charles Edward Peace were caught red handed by the police. Someone who could not be named had been to the police and told them that a robbery was to be carried out at King William dock. There had been three men but unfortunately one managed to slip from the police and got away. The two men had attacked the two night-watchmen, one still in a serious condition. The culprits had a cash box and two barrels of brandy on their persons. The defence was non-existent. Both men had pleaded guilty, hoping for a shorter sentence.

Emma heard the woman behind her speak.

"Someone snitched on them. Who could that have been?"

Emma also wondered who it could have been.

***

The jury was out for thirty minutes. Just time for a pipe of tobacco.

"All stand." The jury returned and gave a guilty verdict. Emma wasn't surprised. Patrick had been foolish. The judge gave his summoning up. He spoke about how evil the two men were and almost killing the two hard working men who were only going about their honest living, something the two defendants wouldn't know about. The woman behind Emma started to sob.

"Charles Edward Peace, I sentence you to twenty years of hard labour."

Patrick took a quick look at Emma.

"Patrick Smith, as far as I am concerned you were the ringleader of this mob and for that I give you twenty-five years hard labour. Constable take them down."

Emma was shocked. Twenty-five years hard labour. The woman behind her shouted profanities at the judge and jury and was dragged outside by the court ushers. Patrick took another look at Emma. It was one of deep sorrow. He shook his head and was led to his fate.

Chapter Twenty-One

Emma was forty-three years old. As she sat at the bare table in her room, she recognised it as a reflection of her life, bare. She had been given more opportunities than most people she had ever known, and yet she had turned her back on it all. Her whole life had been set for destruction.

Emma hadn't anything to take to Kate's. All she had was what she was wearing and the lock of Arthur's hair. Emma had a pleasant surprise when she reached Kate's lodgings. The room was bright with gas mantles on each wall. She knew that Kate was a whore so had expected her to live in a hovel. There was a kitchen range with a fire and a kettle set upon it, a bed in the corner with crisp white sheets. The table had a cloth on it and two china cups and saucers.

"I bought some bath buns to have with our tea," Kate said.

"I thought you might be hungry, so there's an extra one." She pushed the plate towards Emma.

Emma was confused. "Why are you doing this, Kate?"

"I know what Patrick would do to you. He isn't the best of men and you remind me of my mother. She was a lady like you I was told." The young girl took a big bite out of the bath bun.

"There are lots of bad people around these parts. I have to be careful. You could look after me in a motherly sort of way. You could take the money from my customers before they run off, and stay close to me so they don't take advantage. Patrick used to do that for me, now you could take his place.

I know you don't have the brawn, but I'm sure you have the brains."

Emma couldn't agree with Kate. Brains were the last of her assets. Patrick was Kate's pimp. Why didn't she realise that? She thought she was his mistress. Kate pulled the tin bath from the hook on the wall outside and set it down on the rag rug in front of the fire. They heated water in the kettle and pans until there was enough water for Emma to bathe in.

"Here, use this. One of my sailor boys gave it to me - soap with real French perfume in."

Emma stepped into the hot water and slowly immersed herself. She rubbed the soap across her arms and legs. It was sheer luxury. Kate got a jug and poured hot water over Emma's matted hair. She held a sheet out for Emma to dry herself. They sat and drank tea with a dash of gin. Kate took an hour brushing Emma's hair so it no longer looked like a bird's nest.

"Come on I have a beau tonight at eight. It doesn't take long. I can leave you in the Ten Bells with a drink, then I'll meet you."

Emma felt a little strange taking food and shelter from this young girl, but what else could she do?

***

They walked up to the inn. Emma was experiencing a feeling she had not had for a long time - cleanliness. Her hair was combed and fastened up on top of her head, and she wore a borrowed stuff skirt and flannel petticoat. They entered the bar together. Many heads turned to look at them.

"Goodness, is this gay Paris?" The crowd laughed, and they were immediately joined by a crowd of men who bought gin and rum for the women.

"Mrs Smith, I'm sorry about Patrick. He was a good friend to me."

The man was tall and dark. Emma thanked him, but she didn't want to entertain anymore men. Kate went to meet her beau and Emma was left alone with two men, one a clerk, the other a draper. Emma didn't have to worry about money, the two men bought her drinks. At ten o'clock Kate returned to find Emma very drunk.

"Come on, Emma. We need to be going."

"Oh, don't do that. We're just getting merry," the draper protested.

"Not on my time. Unless you have a couple of bob."

"Two shillings. Is that for both of you?" Kate bent forward showing her firm breasts.

"Of course, but just around the back."

Emma had her head full of laughter and gin. The two men didn't argue who had who, they fell out of the tavern door and into the back yard. The draper pinned Emma up against the privy door.

"Come on Emma gal, open your legs."

The man pushed himself into Emma. She gasped as he climaxed almost at once. He pulled away, tottering as he tried to fasten his trousers. Emma felt bruised and nauseous, reeling from what had just happened. Kate was still rocking back and forth with the bank clerk. After they had finished, Kate pulled Emma from the floor and dragged her back to Freeman Street.

"Now how are you feeling? That was lucky wasn't it? Two shillings from them and half a crown from me regular beau."

Emma washed herself carefully and got into the bottom of the bed.

"What's up Emma? You have to take opportunities, don't you? You can't just take from them without them giving something in return. It's the way of the world."

Emma had to admit that this girl had more knowledge of the world than she ever did.

"Oh, my gawd. Didn't Patrick have you working for him?"

"No, I was his wife," Emma said innocently.

"No, you bloody weren't. He was married to a woman near Spitalfields market."

"He can't have been. He gave me a ring. He lived with me."

"Did he live with you all the time?"

Emma realised that he didn't. He would often go for days. Her whole life had been a lie.

"I'm sorry, Kate. I'm confused."

"I don't think you knew much about Patrick, did you?" Kate put her arm around Emma.

"I was twelve years old when he sweet talked me into bed. He was a proper beau, bought trinkets and hair combs. I was living in a cellar with my ten brothers and sisters, working in a warehouse, cleaning bottles from the age of six. I was blessed when Patrick came along. I didn't have to wash bottles again."

"Twelve years old?"

"I'm not ashamed of that. It's not unusual here abouts. There's worse things that could have happened to me. I had a roof over my head, food in my belly and someone to watch over me." She was defiant. Emma was ashamed of Patrick. How could he live off a young girl?

"You're brave, Kate."

She pulled the sheets around them and sang a sweet lullaby.

Chapter Twenty-Two

"Emma, you don't have to work with me. Just keep close so no-one takes advantage."

"I'll be close, don't worry."

On Saturday they went into the market and had chicken with crispy skin then onto the Ten Bells for an afternoon gin. The tavern was quiet. Just two men stood at the bar. The shorter one, dressed in a dark topcoat, kept looking across at Emma. Eventually he came across to them. Emma thought that she recognised him but couldn't remember where from.

"Good afternoon, Mrs Turner." He gave a low bow which made Kate snigger.

"It's Mrs Smith now, sir."

"Oh, I do apologise ma'am. I don't think you remember me. Robert Mann. And my friend here is James Hatfield."

Yes, she remembered now. Old Montague Street Mortuary, where Joseph had been taken.

"We're picking a body up. Some poor soul who has had a terrible accident just like your poor husband."

Emma's flesh was crawling. She felt the gin rise in her throat. The man at the bar didn't move or utter a word. He looked down into his pint of beer.

"Well I shouldn't delay you Mr Mann. Thank you for all you did for my husband and for me." Robert Mann tipped his hat and the two men left.

"Oh gawd. I wouldn't like to meet them on a dark night." Kate poked an elbow into Emma's ribs.

***

Over the next few months Kate and Emma drank, ate and sang together. Emma held Kate's bonnet when she went into the tavern's back yard with a customer and stood outside the room door when she had one of her regulars.

***

One-night Emma was sat in the Ten Bells when Kate had picked up a young man who seemed wet behind the ears. Emma held onto Kate's bonnet as they went around the inn for Kate to perform her service. She was longer than the usual half an hour. With no sign of the couple Emma trod very carefully into the back yard. The gas light was very low and the paving stones slippy. She couldn't see Kate or her customer.

"Kate, where are you?" she whispered at first, her voice rising slightly. There wasn't an answer. Emma sobered up very quickly. She opened the door to the privy. On the grey flagged floor with her stockings and garters showing was Kate, her face beaten to a pulp.

"No Kate, no. Please God no. Help. Someone, help." The landlord came to the back door.

"What's to do?" He rushed to Emma's side and saw the body.

"Bloody Mary, Murder, Murder." He ran into the street to alert the police. There was a whistle then another. Emma clung to the landlord and cried. He took her inside and gave her a large slug of brandy.

"Do you know who she was with?"

"A nice young lad. I haven't seen him before."

One of the police constables told her she could go home, but that tomorrow she should go to Leman Street police station to give a statement.

Emma went back to Kate's room. She had to be quick. She went under the mattress and found Kate's cache - a five-pound note and six shillings, a jet necklace and a ring with tiny seed pearls. The door flew off its hinges and a brute of a man as tall as he was wide took two steps to reach her. He held her by the throat until her feet left the floor.

"So, someone got here before me." He squeezed Emma's throat again.

"What have you there?" he snatched the five pound note out of Emma's hand.

"Who are you?" he shouted into her face. She could smell onions and ale.

"I'm Emma Smith, Patrick Smith's wife." The thug loosened his grip on Emma.

"Paddy's wife?" He looked at her closely.

"Yes, they said he was married to a toff." He took the shillings and the jewellery from her hand and put them in his waistcoat pocket.

"They didn't say that she was a thief though."

"I'm not a thief. I've live here with Kate ever since Patrick was sent to prison. She's dead. She's been killed behind the Ten Bells."

"I know that already. She should have known I wanted me money. That's what happens to those who don't do as they are told. When Patrick got sent down, she was to come to me. It was an agreement. She thought she was too good for me, the little tart." Emma looked at the brute of a man, the tweed jacket he wore seemed too tight and his shirt with no collar made his neck seem as thick as a tree trunk. His boots were heavy with steel toe caps.

"Were you working with her?" He looked deep into her eyes ensuring she told him the truth.

"No, I'm not a whore. She helped me when Patrick couldn't. She was kind to me."

"Very kind my arse. The police will be calling here soon so you need to push off."

Emma didn't want to argue with the man. She left with no hope for her future.

Chapter Twenty-Three

Emma knocked at Kitty's door. George opened it just a crack. He was half asleep.

"Emma, what do you want at this time of night? We're all in bed." Kitty had got up and opened the door wider.

"Emma come in."

When she was fully in the room Emma could see Albert asleep on the two armchairs.

"Please can I sleep here tonight Kitty? Kate has been murdered."

"No, she's not staying here. We've done enough for her."

"George, she needs us." Kitty tried to calm her husband.

"I said no. She always needs us." He was adamant.

"Just tonight please, George."

"I'm going to bed." George saw that it was a useless exercise.

"You'll have to sleep in front of the fire. There isn't anywhere else."

"Anywhere will do. I'm so sorry for coming to your door."

Emma settled down in front of the few embers that shone a light in the grate. Kitty gave her two shawls for bedding and to keep out the cold.

"Thank you, Kitty."

She was asleep in five minutes, exhausted at the night's events.

***

Emma was woken by Albert who started to prepare for work. It was six o'clock. George and Kitty were up five minutes later. Kitty began making breakfast, frying bread in a large black pan. George and Albert set off together while Kitty made tea with a dash of gin. Maude and baby Emma got up, the baby had grown and had long red locks, poor Maude looked worn out with her bundle of trouble. Emma told them all about what had happened, the gruesome murder and the encounter with the thug.

"Who was he, Emma?" Maude's eyes were like saucers.

"I don't know. Some criminal."

"What are you going to do, Emma? I'm sorry but I've promised George that you won't be here when he returns from work."

"I have to go to the police station to give a statement this morning. I'll just have to take it from there."

She started to panic. She really was in the gutter now, but Kitty had done more than enough. She had just outstayed her welcome. Emma walked to the police station on Leman Street. The sergeant on the front desk looked up. "Yes?" His cheeks were bright red.

"My name is Emma Smith, Mrs Emma Smith. I was told to present myself this morning."

"Oh, present yourself?" The Sargent mocked Emma's manner, surprised by this woman he thought was a laundry maid.

The detective dealing with the case took Emma's statement. She told him about the thug in Kate's room.

"Did you know him, or had you seen him before?"

"No, but he did say that Kate had got what was coming to her."

Emma described the thug and what he was wearing. She started to cry. James Alcott felt a little sorry for her. She had more than likely fallen on hard times.

"If you live on Freeman Street, where did you go last night?"

Emma told him she had stayed with a friend in Hope Street.

"There's a place I know that's run by a charitable body on George Street, run by a Mrs Shaw. I can get you a room there if you want. You'll probably have to share though." He watched Emma crumble a little more.

"It's for women who have fallen on hard times."

She smiled back at him. "Thank you, sir."

He wrote down the address and information along with a reference note for the matron.

***

She knocked on the door of number 18 George Street with its scrubbed step and brass numbers nailed to the middle of the door. Emma felt numb. She had no joy in living. She was as her Uncle Charles had said, in the gutter. A stout woman of about fifty opened the door, her hair tied up in a French bun and perched on top was a starched white cap. She wore a black dress with a collar. The woman looked at Emma from the floor upwards.

"Yes?"

Emma handed her the note the detective had given her she couldn't open her mouth, or she would have broken down completely.

"Mrs Smith, come in. You're lucky. We have a bed free."

Emma crossed the threshold.

"Number four, here you are. You'll be sharing with Tilly. She's at work in the market. We do encourage work here. The bed near the window is hers. Come with me."

Emma followed like a small child.

"I'm Mrs Russell the deputy keeper. The front door is locked at ten o'clock. You're not allowed to bring alcohol onto the premises." They entered a very neat parlour.

"This parlour is for residents' use. There should be no eating in here."

Mrs Russell marched Emma to the large kitchen, which housed a range of pots and pans. Twelve chairs were positioned next to a long table and to the end of the kitchen was a walk-in pantry.

"You're not allowed there. I have a key and Mrs Baxter the cook has one. Breakfast is at eight o'clock, supper is at six o'clock. You need to sign in every day with a member of staff. Do you understand? I need you to sign or make your mark on this paper."

Emma signed and felt like a prisoner.

"I just need your details, then I will give you sheets for the bed."

Emma made up the bed. They smelled of roses. She laid on it and hot tears ran down her face. The bed was comfortable, and she was exhausted and was soon sleeping soundly.

***

She was awoken by a heavy hand shaking her.

"Get up. Mrs Russell will have your guts for garters if she catches you on the bed. We're not allowed during the day."

"Oh, I'm sorry. My name is Emma. You must be Tilly."

"Yes, I'm pleased to meet you." Tilly thought that the older woman looked frightened.

"It's all right here Emma. There are lots of rules but none to worry about. Do you like a drink?" She didn't really have to ask. Emma had the hardened face of a regular drinker.

Emma nodded and Tilly went under her pillow and brought out a bottle of gin.

"Here, have a swig. I know how bad it is and it looks like you need some."

Emma thanked her and took a mouthful.

"Good isn't it? Not your barrel stuff proper London gin. So how come you're here?"

The women talked and drank. Emma told her of Patrick going to prison and Kate's murder. She didn't need to know much more. Tilly had been in service, but the master of the house had raped her, so she ran away and someone at the chapel had recommended the charity to her. She had been there over a year. She had a job every morning at the market on Brick Lane. It was seven days a week. She had to pay board now, but she didn't care the house was safe in the dangerous streets of Whitechapel. Emma was feeling much better as the gin found its way through her body.

At six o'clock Tilly and Emma went to the kitchen. Mrs Baxter, the cook, welcomed her, "If you're not working then there are chores to do in the house. You can start with the pots and pans after your supper."

The other six residents joined them at the table. The fish pie was ladled out. Emma was eager to eat. She couldn't remember when she last had a good meal.

"Steady, slow down, Emma." Tilly rested a hand on her roommate's arm.

"Sorry, please excuse me. It's a wonderful meal." Mrs Baxter puffed up with pride.

"Well there's a delicious rice pudding for afters."

She thought the new woman had excellent manners. All the women helped to clear the dishes and to wash them.

"I think I'll go for a walk if that's all right," Emma said to Tilly.

"We're not in prison, Emma. You're allowed to go out, but don't be late back. Mrs Russel is hot on the clock and if you're in after-hours three times, you're thrown out."

Emma reassured her that she wouldn't be late, but she needed a drink. She didn't have any money. She would have to beg for it or find a man who would buy her a glass or two. She went to the Britannia and sat with a group of the women she knew. They knew she was in a bad way with her husband being locked up and her friend murdered. A woman called Mary gave her a glass of gin which Emma sipped to make it last the evening.

Emma's eyes rested on those of Robert Mann. He stood at the bar and nodded acknowledging her. She nodded back. Her eyes were firmly stuck to the tavern floor, she could feel her skin crawl. A chill ran down her body and she got closer to the woman at the side of her. He was alone, his tall friend nowhere to be seen. Emma made fun with one of the girls and the laughter ran around the room. Robert Mann now sat on the next table. She shuffled into her seat so she didn't have to look at him.

"Mrs Smith, it's nice to see you again. You're all a merry bunch."

Emma smiled but didn't want to join in the conversation.

"You look as though you need your glass replenishing. Allow me."

Emma was about to say no, but the need for the drink took over.

"Thank you, sir. You're most kind."

Robert Mann went to the bar and came back with a large glass of gin. She said thank you and took a mouthful immediately.

"I've been on business for one of the professors at the hospital. I am a trusted person at the mortuary."

Emma didn't care. He was repulsive to her. The mantle clock struck nine. Emma became flustered.

"Oh, I have to go my new lodgings. They have a time rule. Please, sir, I need to go."

He understood perfectly being in the workhouse there was a time rule of nine o'clock, although he had special dispensation because of his post as mortuary assistant.

"That is very regrettable Mrs Smith. We can meet on another day though." He said hopefully.

"Yes, sir. Please, I must leave."

He moved his legs to allow her to go. She fastened her bonnet and ran down the street.

***

Tilly was already in bed.

"Goodnight Emma. Sleep tight."

"Good night, Tilly. God bless."

Emma snuggled down between the clean sheets. She was lucky to be here. Two minutes later she was fast asleep.

***

Emma started to work at the market on a weekend with Tilly. She sold pints of cockles and mussels from a barrow. The smell on her hands was impregnated with the scent of fish, but at least she was able to pay for her gin habit. She still frequented the Ten Bells and gave her favours now and again if she felt safe enough. Nothing mattered any more. She was void of feelings. Men were all animals, all but Joseph of course. Sometimes when a sailor was breathing heavily over her breasts, she tried to picture Joseph, then would smell the stale liquor and realised it couldn't be him. She didn't think about what had happened to Kate because she was driven by the liquor. Robert Mann often stood at the bar with his work partner James Hatfield. He would try to buy her drinks or engage in conversation. Emma would make up some excuse or say that she was just going.

Chapter Twenty-Four
3rd April, 1888

Emma had finished her chores and was quickly out to The Ten Bells. It was cold. You could feel the frost crisp in the air. Spring had not yet warmed the murky night air. Gas lamps flickered and Emma pulled her shawl around herself. She really needed to cut the drink down.

There was a chance that she might have a full-time job in the market. No more lifting her skirts for lonely sailors or drunken clerks. She could hear the throng inside the tavern before she got to the door. The singing sounded like someone strangling a cat. As she opened the front door, Robert Mann's eyes met hers. Her heart sank. He nodded and turned to James Hatfield and whispered something to him.

"Emma dearie. Come and sit down yourself here," a woman said.

Emma joined the group of cackling whores and ordered a pennyworth of gin. The landlord gave one of his best customers a peck on the cheek as he placed the glass in front of her.

"Don't be cheeky," she joked with him. He had a special place in her heart since the murder of Kate. He'd been kind in so many ways. Robert Mann had his back to the bar, resting his elbows.

"She's a grand woman, James." His eyes took in all of

Emma.

"No point looking. She ain't going to have 'owt to do with you."

James Hatfield didn't look at Emma, he looked into the bottom of his empty glass.

"She's like a real lady."

"She's a tuppenny whore like the rest of them harlots."

James wasn't interested in Emma. His experience of women wasn't a good one. He'd been married twice and they had both died on him. One had a wicked tongue which he had to chastise on many occasions, one of the times being when he had hit her so hard, she fell backwards and banged her head hard on the brass fender, killing her outright. The last one died in childbirth, no consideration for him.

"She's taking you for a fool Robert. Quick to take your money but slow to open her thighs." Robert Mann was angry with his friend but went over to Emma.

"Mrs Smith, a pleasant evening I'm sure."

"It is indeed, Mr Mann." Emma was polite and to the point.

He rubbed his hands together. "Would you allow me to buy you a glass of porter or gin?"

She tried to let him down gently and didn't want to feel obliged to speak to him.

"Thank you, Mr Mann. You're very kind, but it isn't necessary."

"Please let me buy you a glass. No obligations."

"I'll take a glass of porter then, Mr Mann." He went to the bar and paid for it.

"You're a fool, Robert."

"I'll have her against the privy wall before the night's out."

James Hatfield let his sombre face crack as he laughed at him and took a sip of the lukewarm ale.

He bowed to Emma. "Here we are your ladyship. One glass of the house's finest porter."

She thought he was too familiar with her, but she smiled and the women around her made tittering noises.

"Emma's got a beau," said Cider Sally

Emma's face flushed, and she kicked Sally under the table. Robert Mann thought that it was one mark for him. As the night progressed, Robert Mann filled Emma's glass, she became very drunk and he thought she was prime for the picking.

"Now my dear, maybe I could walk you back to your lodgings. There's many a dangerous blaggard about Whitechapel on a night."

"I think not, Mr Mann. I'm well on my own."

"You've emptied my pockets, Mrs Smith."

"No sir, no. You have emptied your pocket freely."

Robert Mann breathed hard through his nose. He had been made to look the fool in front of the whole of the tavern. Even James was smirking at her rebuff. He went to the bar and got hold of his friend before leaving the tavern. All the women laughed. Emma was relieved that he had gone. She could imagine what he wanted and there was no way that she was going to lift her skirts for him. She checked the mantle clock and said her goodbyes to the rowdy bunch of women.

"Be careful, Emma," shouted Sally.

Emma waved and wrapped her shawl tightly around herself.

***

There was someone coughing in the fog. It was a pea-souper coming up from the river, the hazy gas light made eerie shadows on the pavement. Emma heard the clip-clopping of a cart horse and the wheels of the cart it was pulling. She was unsteady on her feet and had had more than enough tonight. Robert Mann was getting above his station thinking that he could take her home. The horse clopped past her but stopped at the corner of Brick Lane. Emma saw the driver get down and go to the back of the cart. She carried on past them. Suddenly, a pair of hands got hold of her. It was useless to try and struggle.

"Please sir, I am a poor woman. I haven't got anything."

What she thought was a coal sack was put over her head

and she was thrown to the floor. She tried to scream but any sound was muffled by the sack. She twisted and turned trying to get free then realised that there was more than one attacker. There was a pair of hands on her shoulders and another at her feet. Then she understood what was going to happen. A voice whispered into her ear.

"Free with everything you tart."

Emma squirmed. Her skirt and underskirts were pulled above her waist and she felt the cold air hit her belly. Then she screamed with pain as a hand was thrust inside her. She screamed again and again, and heard another voice.

"You hold 'er legs. I want a feel."

Her position was turned, and another molesting hand was rammed inside her. She vomited inside the sack.

"Pass the driving stick."

There was shuffling, and the horse moved a little making its shoe strike the cobble.

"No, please God. no." Emma screamed for her life, but no-one came to help.

The driving stick was thrust with hatred. Emma made one last scream then lost consciousness. The night air rippled across her body and Emma regained consciousness. There was a dull pain deep in her body. She crawled on her hands and knees to 18 George Street. She tried the door but it was locked. She knocked on the window and Tilly pulled back the curtain. Tilly could see Emma holding her belly and that she was in deep distress. Tilly had been to Mrs Russell who unlocked the door firstly to reprimand Emma, but she was not prepared for the sight that met her.

Emma was laid on her bed, her face covered with coal dust. She had blood running down her legs. Tilly gently lifted her skirts. Both women stood back in horror, shocked at the sight they were met with. Already great bruises were forming on her thighs with finger-marks imprinted in Emma's pale flesh.

"Who did this to you, Emma?" asked Mrs Russell.

"Two, three men. I don't know. Please help me."

"We will my girl. Tilly help me. I'm taking Emma to the

hospital."

Tilly wiped blood from Emma's legs then wrapping her own shawl about the poor woman.

They walked to the London Hospital. Mrs Russell and Tilly at either side of Emma assisted her along the way. Emma wasn't crying anymore. She was strangely quiet. At the hospital, two nurses took care of her. Tilly was sent back to George Street, but Mrs Russell stayed. The doctor examined Emma, then went to speak to Mrs Russell. Emma had been through a terrible ordeal, her peritoneum had been ruptured with a blunt object and she was at risk of peritonitis. It was life threatening. Mrs Russell sat at her bedside. Emma opened her eyes. She looked at Mrs Russell. She wasn't going to die alone.

"I'm glad you're awake. You're going to be all right."

Emma closed her eyes and whispered. "Victoria."

"Who is Victoria? Do you have a sister? A daughter?"

Emma didn't open her eyes again. At nine o'clock in the morning Emma Elizabeth Smith was pronounced dead.

***

The inquest was held on the 7th April, 1888. The local inspector of the Metropolitan Police, Edmund Reid, informed the coroner that Emma Smith had said she was attacked by two or three men and that one could have been a youth. Due to her condition there had been no other information to hand. The deceased was a prostitute and market worker. Some say she had a cultured accent.

Robert Mann and James Hatfield sat in the coroner's court as they had received the body of the deceased into old Montague Street mortuary. James Hatfield sat on the bench, listening as the injuries to the body were read aloud. He leant over to Robert who was at the side of him.

"She got what she deserved. What do you say?" he whispered.

"They all deserve it. Dirty whores the lot of them."

***

Inquest for Emma Smith, 4th April 1888.
The Duty Surgeon Dr. Hillier.

Report: A blunt object had been inserted into her vagina rupturing her peritoneum.
Coroner: Wynne Edwin Baxter.
Verdict: Murder by person or persons unknown.

Annie Millwood

Chapter Twenty-Five

It was the darkest of days. The fog had come out in sympathy with Annie. Her heart had been shattered into a thousand pieces. She put her hand into the wooden box and grabbed a handful of wet earth. Edward, Richard's brother, had managed an hour from his desk to pay his respects. He followed behind Annie using the vicar's silver spoon, not wanting to get his hands dirty, even for his brother. Edward had explained to Annie that his wife had been unable to attend the funeral as she had a chill and that she was such a delicate creature.

"Well I need to get back to Fawcett and Millwood. I'm sorry I can't stay any longer."

He brushed his gloves of any offending material. He looked at Annie from her boots to her bonnet. She could feel his disgust seeping from every pore. Edward was uncomfortable with the situation as Edward liked to call it. His dead brother had left a young wife and daughter who was feeble-minded without a penny piece.

"You're in a dreadful situation," Edward said again.

Annie knew clearly how bad it was. She couldn't see how she was going to pay for the funeral. Richard had been a hardworking man but had a serious illness. The doctors couldn't treat him. He was losing weight because he was unable to eat anything. Richard had written to his brother begging him to help his family. He asked Edward to pay the rent and living expenses until he was able to return to work.

Richard and Annie's daughter, Sarah, was a delicate child and didn't have a full mental capacity. Annie didn't have a job as Richard had always provided for them and Sarah needed full time care. The day progressed with a downpour.

"Annie, I must speak to you about finances."

Annie looked at him blankly.

"I presume you don't have the money to pay for the funeral."

"No, I don't Edward." He had made her feel desperate in just one sentence.

To Edward's horror, Annie began to cry. Sarah, upset that her mother was crying, started to weep herself. Her brother-in-law had not approved of the marriage between Richard and Annie and blamed them for the early demise of his mother, who had shut herself away with grief at Richards insistence at marrying Annie. She had threatened to disinherit him, but he ignored her and married Annie, whom he loved dearly. The brothers had fallen out, they had met on a few occasions but their friendship as young brothers had never been the same. Edward had married the boss's daughter Lucille Fawcett. She had visited her father's offices and taken a fancy to him. They lived in a leafy part of London with a carriage at their disposal and maids of all work. Lucille's father didn't want his beautiful daughter getting her hands dirty. It wasn't long before Edward was given a partnership, enabling them to live very comfortably.

"I thought you would not be able to pay. I'll arrange with the funeral directors to send the account to me and then I'll clear the debt. I'd also like to provide for Sarah. She needs full-time care and attention and I'm sure you'll have to find full-time employment to earn some money."

His face was grey. He stared at the floor not wanting to make eye contact with Annie.

"I'm the chairman of the London Asylum. I can assure you that Sarah will be very well looked after with lots of activities. She would thrive there."

Annie didn't want to lose Sarah but there wasn't an alternative at this time, and if Edward was the chairman

Sarah was bound to receive the best of care. Annie nodded.

"Thank you, Edward." She could have choked on the words.

***

The following week Sarah and Annie met Edward at the sanatorium. The hospital was set in manicured gardens a bandstand and inmates playing croquet on the lawn. Annie was pleased with the place. It was something they were unable to afford. There were easels set up and inmates painting and drawing something Sarah loved. The matron made them feel welcome and encouraged Sarah to paint a picture. Tea was made, then a nurse took Sarah away. Annie wanted to drag her daughter away and run, but she knew this was the best option for her. Sarah would be fed and have a roof over her head - something Annie was not in a position to do. The matron said a report would be sent to Edward every month explaining the treatment and the welfare of the patient. Annie wondered why the report would not be sent to her. The matron very kindly informed her that the person paying for the care would be the only person privy to the reports of the progress of the patient.

Chapter Twenty-Six

Annie went home exhausted by the trauma of losing her husband and now her daughter. Edward had made it very clear that he would not be supporting Annie. He had paid her rent for a month, then advised her to find cheaper accommodation along with employment. He thought he had done his duty towards his brother, was a good uncle looking after his niece, but Annie was unwanted baggage and he was not prepared to take her on. It was 1886 and life was hard for a woman on her own. Annie found a cheap lodging house at Spitalfields Chambers, 8 Whites Row. The room was contaminated with vermin. There was a cast iron bed in the corner with a chamber pot for under the bed, the mattress was of straw and had many bodies imprinted on it. The room had no cooking facilities apart from a small grate to boil a kettle. She had to eat from the food barrows on the streets of Whitechapel. Over the next few weeks Annie had a diet of bread and dripping with a cup of rice milk or a cup of tea. A neighbour of Annie's advised her of a job going at the Three Compasses on Whitechapel High Street. She brushed her hair and tidied herself. Angus the landlord, a great hairy man who would throw grown men into the street if they caused trouble in his hostelry, felt a little sorry for Annie after hearing her tale. His mother had been a widow, so it touched his well-hidden heart. He gave Annie ten minutes of training on how to pull the ale and which glass to use for each drink, and she was told in no uncertain terms, not to spill a drop.

"Profit, Annie. Each drop spilt is profit." He enforced this statement by slamming the table.

The tavern was always full, selling ale, gin and porter to the rabble of London. Annie's duties included cleaning the tables, washing the glasses and stoking the fires. A young soldier chancing his arm slapped Annie's backside.

"Whotcha!" she said, moving swiftly.

"Come on dearie. Give us a kiss."

"Not likely. Keep your bloody hands to yourself." Annie didn't mind the bit of fun, but she didn't want to be classed as one of the prostitutes that frequented such taverns in the area.

"I have a shilling," he said hopefully.

"Not for me, sir. But I'm sure there will be a lady out there for you to spend your money on."

His friends all laughed. Prostitution was rife. Every woman in the area had been part of it at some time or other in their lives. Annie had been lucky so far as not to have to sink to that level. She had been married with a husband who had earned enough to support their family because he didn't drink his wages away. However, she didn't rule out prostitution. It might be necessary and if needs must. Annie was missing her daughter. Unfortunately the asylum was too far away to walk to, and she didn't have the money for an omnibus. Her wages didn't go far and, because there was no kitchen range, most of her food was bought from the barrows - a half penny hot potato or a penny pie. She would use the same tea leaves for six cups of tea until it looked clear. The customers in the bar were friendly, the ale and gin flowed freely. Customers would buy her drinks for a friendly smile. One regular called after work every day. He was tall with whiskers, quite handsome with a lovely smile. He always cheered her up. He asked about her wellbeing and it wasn't long before she was telling him her life story. She, in turn, listened to his life and how he had ended up in London. They were both people that needed another soul.

"What time do you finish, Annie?"

"What's it to you?" she asked.

"I thought you might be a little hungry after your shift.

You must need a bite."

She thought there couldn't be any harm, and she was starving to death. But more than that. She needed to be with someone. She had missed the interactions with Sarah. She just needed to touch another human being.

"I finish at eleven o'clock. An early night tonight. I'll meet you outside."

Peter Roberts was a warehouse man, never married but with his fair share of women in the past. He had been watching her for weeks. She had felt his eyes following her about the bar. He thought she was a hard worker and that she didn't put up with any nonsense from her customers. He also noticed that Annie wasn't free with her favours like the other women that worked in the tavern.

Peter stood nervously outside waiting for Annie running his fingers through his thick brown hair. Annie pulled her shawl around her body as the wind was keen. They walked down to the pie shop; Annie's mouth-watering at the smell of food. There was a great menu written on the white tiled wall.

"Have what you want Annie."

Annie couldn't decide. She wanted it all then quietly said, "I'll have the pudding and peas please."

"Certainly."

Peter ordered a pork pie for himself. They sat at a rickety table in the corner of the shop and there was an uncomfortable silence until the food arrived. Annie wolfed down the food.

"Steady on, gal."

He was astonished at how fast she ate the black pudding. He thought she must have been starving and asked if she wanted some more.

"No, I'm all right. It's just I haven't eaten today."

Peter pushed his plate towards her with the remains of his pie.

"What you need is a man to look after you."

Annie stopped eating. "Well maybe I do, but the right one hasn't come along. Was that an offer?"

"Could be. What do you say?"

"I think you're a bit eager."

She looked at him. He must have been the same age as her, could have a much younger woman than her. He was a bit of a catch - clean, and with a job.

"I suppose we could get to know each other." Her heart was melting.

"Yes, I would be happy to do that."

They shook hands as though they had done a deal, then Peter leant over and kissed her. She didn't stop him. Annie thought it was good to have a man close to her again. She turned over and kissed Peter. He'd been gentle with her. Richard had been the only man she had ever made love to this was a new experience.

There was a chink in the curtains which threw a weak beam of light across the room. She looked around. The place was miserable, mould growing in the corners, the oil cloth cracked and worn. But what could she do about it?

She turned in the straw bed towards Peter. She could smell his body the aroma of the tavern and a faint smell of cedarwood. He awoke and turned towards her, smiled and pulled her body closer to him, kissing her softly on the neck then her breasts. She lay blissfully happy as he explored her with his lips.

Chapter Twenty-Seven

After a few weeks, Peter suggested he move in with Annie. He was living in a working men's hostel on Whitechapel Road, but was now spending more time with her, and she couldn't say no to him. He arrived at six-thirty with an armful of belongings wrapped in brown paper. He had a piece of sheeting, two white collars, a Sunday shirt, a pair of woollen socks, a packet of boot laces and a mantle clock. The clock had been in his family for years. It didn't work as he had over wound it, but he'd promised when he had enough money he would take it for repair.

Peter told Annie his family had lived in Kent. His mother and father had passed away so he thought he would take a chance of earning a living in London. He had been in and out of work, taking whatever came his way. The landlady said she would charge an extra sixpence a week for Peter staying. Annie was happy for the first time in a year, they couldn't make plans because money was scarce, but they had dreams most outrageous, but it gave them an escape from the slums they were living in.

Angus the landlord asked Annie to get Peter to move from the bar, other customers had complained that Annie was talking to Peter and ignoring them. Peter didn't take the request well and sulked in a corner. It wasn't like him, but there was that little bit of jealousy rearing its ugly head. Annie felt strangely pleased and flattered. That feeling didn't last for long. Annie was able to handle the jokes and lewd comments. It went with the job. But Peter began to get involved in minor brawls, trying to protect Annie's honour.

"That's it, Peter. You're barred," Angus shouted. He hated fighting as it brought the peelers to the door.

"Oh, Angus. No." Annie begged him not to bar Peter.

"I can't have it. It always happens when the barmaids get fellas. He's out."

Peter waited outside. He was nursing a black eye and a cut lip.

"I'm sorry, Peter. He won't let you back in."

"Then you need to finish. I can't let you work there with that bunch of scum."

"Peter, I can't give my job up. We need the money."

She could tell that he was furious. His face was set and he was breathing down his nose, furious at what had happened. Annie walked behind him like a dog feeling the heat of his anger. Reaching their room, he put his jacket on the end of the bed then turned quickly and punched Annie straight in the face.

"Why do you have to argue with me? Why wouldn't you do what I have asked?"

"I don't know what you mean Peter," she cried.

"Don't give me that, woman. You wanted me out of the tavern so you can carry on with every uniformed man in London. I've seen you looking at them."

"No, I only want you Peter. Truly I do."

She pleaded with him, feeling the blood flow down her face.

"You promised me."

His face touched hers. She could feel his hot breath on her cheek.

"Yes, you're the only man for me."

Her throat constricted with the sobs that she was trying not to release.

"I'm sorry for hurting you, Annie. Please forgive me?"

Annie's father had been strict, but he had never hit her. Richard had been a gentle soul. No man had ever hit or even raised their hand to her before. She wasn't stupid though she knew she had to make him feel secure. Peter got a cloth and bathed Annie's eye, whispering sweet words into her ear. He told her to put her shawl on. They walked arm in arm down the street to the hot potato man. Peter took morsels of potato and attempted to feed Annie. She moved her head away then he tried again, and she saw the flicker of anger in his eye and accepted it willingly. Then he was back to his usual self. Annie wasn't interested in their love-making that night, but Peter was satisfied and rolled away and fell asleep quickly. She climbed out of bed and wrapped her shawl about her chilled body. Annie reached for the bottle of gin. It was bitter, but she needed to take the taste of hatred away from her heart.

Peter carried on the next day as though nothing had happened and when Annie finished work at the tavern at midnight, he was waiting for her. He was unsteady on his feet but was smiling and held a bunch of cornflowers.

"For my princess."

He kissed her cheek and she responded by kissing him back.

"Thank you, kind sir."

They ate sausages and roasted onions from the brazier at the corner of the street. Annie tried to dismiss what had happened the night before as something that wasn't going to happen again, but deep in her stomach she felt uneasy. Annie was on her early shift the next week. She would be in work at six o'clock in the morning serving breakfast to the travellers that were staying in the inn. She then had to build fires and scrub floors to prepare to open for the customers.

Peter went to work but wanted to know what she was doing after she had finished work, and she reluctantly gave him a list of her chores she had to do in their room. He told her to meet at The Ten Bells at six-thirty that evening. Annie stood outside of the tavern as Peter strolled down the street covered in dust. The bar was full, and they pushed through the crowd to order drinks. A noisy crowd sat around an empty grate. There was a man with a monkey on a chain sat in the corner. The monkey jumped and did somersaults to the delight of onlookers. Peter drank ale and Annie had a glass of mother's ruin. They sat in silence watching the free spectacle before them. Annie could feel the tension building between them. She didn't want to talk to him but knew if she didn't say anything, things would get out of hand. It was then that a clumsy idiot fell onto the table and Peter immediately jumped up to confront the man.

"Hey, watch it you fool. Our drinks."

"Looks to me you've had enough already," the man answered.

Peter jumped up and took a swing before landing a punch on the man's jaw. The landlord came from behind the bar and gave them a talking to. Peter clenched his fists as though he was going to tackle the landlord next but thought better. Instead he took hold of Annie's wrist, dragging her from her seat.

"We're off." Her arms and legs hit every table on the way out.

"Bastards. Bloody fools. It wasn't my fault."

"No. It wasn't, my love," she said as they stood on the pavement outside.

Peter made a small sound in his throat, "You don't mean that do you? I'm the fool aren't I?"

He was holding her wrists tightly, making her wince.

"It wasn't your fault Peter," she pleaded to him.

Annie tried to prepare for what was about to happen. The back of Peter's hand hit her cheek. Men jeered at him from across the road.

"Leave her alone," a woman shouted, but nobody went to her assistance.

He kicked the back of her legs while he still held onto her wrists. His steel toe capped boots made the muscles on her legs go into spasms. He dragged her down the street until they reached the lodging house. In their room he kicked and punched her to the floor. The beating only lasted a few minutes, Annie curling into a ball trying to protect herself. Peter took his belt from his trousers to whip her frail body.

Annie lost consciousness for a moment and when she

came to, Peter had gone to bed. She could just make out the bed and table as dawn approached. Her body was racked with pain. She didn't think that she deserved such a beating. She pulled herself from the floor and the body in the bed spoke.

"Come to bed, Annie. I need you."

She undressed, feeling every bruise on her body. Peter pulled the blanket over them and climbed on top of her broken body. He performed the act with little response from her.

An hour later she walked into the tavern.

Chapter Twenty-Eight

Angus took one look at her and his mouth fell open.
"What the bloody hell happened?"
"I don't know what you mean."
She tried to smooth her hair.
"Go into the back and look at the mirror in the hallway."
She went into the back and stood on her tip toes to look at her face. The reflection was not of anyone she knew. Her face was contorted into something from a penny dreadful. A swollen eye, a misshapen nose, lips cracked with dried blood on them. He had done a good job on her.
"Did Pete do this?"
"I made him angry."
"Bloody pig. You're not working here today. You need to go home and tidy yourself up, and if he does this to you again, you're finished. I can't have my customers being put off their beer. And you can tell him from me if I see him again, I'll beat his arse."
Annie was horrified that she may lose her job. She hoped Peter had gone to work. She didn't know how much more she could take. She was glad that she didn't own a mirror. If she had seen her face before she'd left for work, she might have taken it up with Peter and then ended up dead. Then she thought how he had made love to her after doing so much damage to her body. In the evening, when Peter arrived home from work, she told him she had been sent home and what Angus had said about more bruises. She didn't tell him about Angus beating his arse. To Peter this was just what he had

wanted. Annie would be sacked from her job and she would have to stay in the room all day.

It was two weeks later when Angus had to let her go. Annie cried and begged him to no avail. Her life was spiralling out of control. Peter had gotten his own way. She was marooned in the room all day while he was at work. One day she was sat on the floor watching the mice run around the room she questioned why she might bother being alive at all, Sarah was cared for, she wasn't in need of anything. She was barely existing. She was destitute and reliant on a brute of a man. Then her mind became dark. There had to be something that she could do.

She waited a short while for Peter to be in a better frame of mind.

"Have you got a spare couple of coppers to buy a preparation to kill the mice? We're infested with the creatures."

He gladly handed over four pennies, pleased she was in an amiable mood. She was a regular customer at the chandlers. She would buy poison for the vermin and candles for the room. Annie imagined that one day they would all be swallowed up by the rats who ran freely in Whitechapel.

Thomas weighed the white powder out and put it in a three-cornered bag. On the way home she felt at peace. She knew what she had to do, and she didn't care.

Peter arrived home in good spirits and they walked hand in hand to The Britannia. They watched a fight between two washer women who were arguing about a pair of trousers. It ended with the trousers being ripped down the middle. The audience stood around then threw lumps of mud at the scratching, hair-pulling harlots. After the tavern, Peter went to bed and she sat on the floor listening to the barking dogs and the music from a screeching violin. Annie tried to make out the tune they were playing and started to hum along with it. She took the poison from the pocket in her petticoat. Slowly she unravelled the paper bag. She wondered what it was going to taste of. She felt sorry for the poor mice. It didn't have a smell. She wondered why. Annie went to the cupboard. There was a chunk of bread, half a pot of dripping and a jug of rice milk. She put a small pile of powder on the second shelf then, taking a quick look at the bed and the sleeping body, put a teaspoon of powder in the rice milk. She stirred until it had dissolved.

Peter rose early for work. Annie made a gravestone of bread and dripping and poured him a cup of rice milk.

"I think that's going off, Annie. It tastes sour." She sniffed at the jug with a look of concern. "Oh I'm sorry, dearie. Do you want me to get more?"

He delved into his pocket and offered her a shilling.

"Get some, and a jug of ale for later. I'll meet you at the White Hart at half past six. And brush your hair. You look a mess."

Annie shopped in the morning, buying rice milk and a jug of ale, a small piece of cheese and a loaf of bread. She drank a cup of the ale and stirred another teaspoon of poison into the rice milk. When Annie got to the tavern, Peter was waiting at the door. He didn't look too well.

"What's wrong, my love? You look pale."

"I feel unwell. We'll just have one, then I'm off to bed."

Annie thought he had a green pallor.

Peter ordered a brandy for himself and a glass of porter for Annie. After throwing the brandy to the back of his throat he held his stomach, then jumped from his seat to go outside. She followed him into Whitechapel Road where she could smell the vomit as it purged from his guts. The pavement was covered. Peter held his stomach as he retched again.

"Come take me home my love."

She put her arm around him and helped him to his bed, returning soon after with a cup of the fresh milk.

"Here we are. That will settle your belly."

He sipped the milk, and, for a few minutes, he closed his eyes, then he vomited the milk across the bed.

"I'm done for, Annie."

"No, you're not. You must have had something bad to eat, that sausage you had yesterday. I said it didn't smell too good, didn't I?"

"You're right. I remember. Give me another drink."

He took a sip of the milk then fell asleep exhausted.

Annie cleared up the mess and smiled. She hadn't reckoned on the poison working so quickly.

Peter's illness got worse over the following few days. He struggled to get to work every day and, on returning in the evening, he didn't eat anything, instead he just drank the rice milk. The stench of the vomit had impregnated his clothes. He started shivering and complaining of the cold.

When he was paid on the Saturday, he went to the quack doctor on Brick Lane who thought it was possible, from his symptoms, that he had the cholera. Annie took him to the London hospital. They treated him for a week and he seemed to recover slightly. When he arrived home he was very weak and unable to raise his fists to Annie. The paper bag was almost empty, but Annie dare not go to the Chandlers' again for more. She had to use what she had wisely. Annie bought some hot oats from the café and mixed the poison in. She wasn't sorry for the way he was. Annie wanted him to feel the pain as she had felt the pain from his beatings. Peter was like a clockwork toy, getting up, going to work, then returning to bed. Weaker men would have stopped work but Annie had to admire his resilience.

It took two more weeks before Peter collapsed at work onto the warehouse floor. A message was sent to the lodging house that he was in Whitechapel mortuary. Annie tidied herself up and went to inquire about him. The small building that was the mortuary had a bell above the door. She could hear it ringing inside. The door was pulled open by a man in a white coat. Annie thought it was the doctor.

"Yes, mum. Can I help you?"

"My friend has been brought in from his works. I'm the only friend he has. I thought I should take his belongings."

The man looked Annie up and down. He introduced himself as Robert Mann, mortuary assistant and working that day with him was James Hatfield.

"Are you dealing with the funeral arrangements, ma'am?"

"No, no. I'm just a friend."

Robert Mann didn't believe her. Annie didn't want to be left with the bill for the funeral.

"Well if no one claims the body after forty-eight hours they are given a paupers burial or sent to the hospital for dissection."

Annie thought the latter would be good enough for Peter. But she wanted to make sure that he was dead and to take any money he had in his pocket.

"Do you want to see the body?" he whispered in her ear.

"Yes, if its permitted."

"It is if I permit it. Have you seen a dead body before?"

"Yes, my husband died not so long ago."

Robert Mann seemed to smile, the corners of his mouth curling at the edges.

"Come through then ma'am, James get number five out." He shouted to his tall friend.

"By the way, if you ain't claiming the body, you can't get his belongings."

Annie nodded and said she understood. The wooden gurney holding Peter's body was splattered with blood. Great black flies buzzed about the room. Annie could feel her stomach heaving.

Robert Mann lifted the grey sheet. Yes, it was Peter. He looked as though he was asleep apart from a little white foam at the corner of his mouth. Annie went to wipe it away.

"No touching the body. It isn't allowed," snapped James Hatfield.

"Forgive me sir," she said.

Her mind was in turmoil. Why didn't she have any compassion for him? Was she so hard? He had got what he deserved.

She left Old Montague Street happy, but she needed to eat. She went to the tavern and spoke to Angus. He agreed to take her back but on shorter hours. Another woman had taken her full time job. Her wage was enough to cover her rent, but there wouldn't be enough to buy food. Angus was pleased Peter had kicked the bucket and gave her two shillings to help her out. She bought half a bottle of gin, a loaf of bread, and a mug of dripping. It was one of the happiest days she had spent in the room.

When Annie was working there was a continuous stream of liquor. It made life bearable. It was then that she decided to join the many women of Whitechapel selling their wares. The first time was a young soldier who asked her if she would join him for some supper after her shift, and she thought, why not, she was starving. She knew she would have to pay for her supper one way or another. The lad was drunk. They left the tavern and wobbled together to the jellied eel barrow. It took Annie less than a minute to polish them off.

"Come on, gal. Haven't you got a kiss for me?"

"Course I have, sweetheart."

He leant over and gave her a fishy kiss.

"Oh, you taste lovely. Give us another."

"That depends. I want my sixpence first."

She had learnt from the women in the tavern to always get your money before the act. Then there isn't an argument later. The soldier gave her a silver sixpence from his waistcoat pocket and she secreted it in her petticoat.

"We need some privacy. I don't want to be on full show."

They went down a dark passageway where the gas lighting was poor and the shadows were places for secret meetings.

"It's fine here."

She wasn't too sure what she was supposed to do, but the lad seemed to have been down an alleyway with a girl before. They stood in a doorway away from the hustle and bustle of Whitechapel Road and prying eyes. He was eager and had dropped his trousers before Annie had lifted her petticoats. He pushed his way into Annie, banging her head on the door behind her.

"Steady boy," she laughed. It was a ridiculous situation.

It lasted a couple of minutes and hadn't been such a traumatic event for her. Peter had raped her most nights. She had always expected it. At that moment there was no relationship, no hate, no regrets, or revenge, just a business arrangement between two people. The young lad fell over his trousers and she helped him up. They left the dark alley and went back to the busy street. He bought her a rosy red apple for her breakfast. She gave him one last kiss and made her way home. She got into bed feeling good about herself and feeling safe. Her new career was now part of life.

Annie would eye someone up in the tavern, then made sure supper was offered as well as her fee. Most days were looked after when she was working. But she needed to expand her business, to save a little money to be able to visit Sarah and take her a little present.

After working extra for two weeks she had saved a few shillings. On the Sunday she washed and brushed her hair. She realised her clothes were not very clean but what could she do about it? Angus had said that he would take her to the asylum, but she would have to find her own way home. The horse and cart rumbled over the cobble stones and Annie was jostled about on the front seat. She was so excited. She couldn't stop talking, Angus had to tell her to be quiet as his ears hurt.

Chapter Twenty-Nine

The main gates were open at the asylum. On Sundays the asylum was open to the public; the Victorians found it therapeutic to wander around the grounds and look at the unfortunates. Angus dropped Annie off at the top of the driveway and she wandered down to the double doors which were ajar. The great hall and reception room had beautiful chairs and tables. A nurse met her. She sniffed a little and asked what Annie wanted. Annie asked for Sarah.

"I don't have you on the list of visitors."

"But I'm her mother, Mrs Millwood."

"I do have a Mr and Mrs Millwood."

"That will be her uncle and aunt."

Annie started to panic. She was a little out of her depth. She knew the nurse didn't approve of her and was frightened that she was going to be thrown out.

"I didn't know you were coming today."

Annie turned quickly. It was Edward with Lucille, looking every inch like wealthy gentry.

"I have scrimped and saved to come to see Sarah. I want to see my daughter."

She didn't stamp her foot, but she felt like doing it.

"Oh, Edward. Please introduce us."

Lucille stepped forward.

"This is Richard's widow, Annie."

Lucille extended her gloved hand and Annie took it.

"How do you do Lucille? I've heard many good things

about you. I'd like to thank you for all you have done for Sarah and myself." Lucille smiled.

She felt ultimately superior to Annie and looked at her from top to toe. Annie pushed a curl back under her bonnet which was black with a bow to the chin. It wasn't fashionable, but it was all she had. It was far from the outfit that Lucille was dressed in, her boots were of kid leather and fastened by small pearl buttons, her dress, matching her coat, was of the highest fashion. At her neck was a jet necklace and finally on her head was a magnificent hat with satin, feathers, lace and net. Edward was uncomfortable. He put his finger in his starched collar as though it was choking him. He didn't want the staff to know that he was in any way related to this ragamuffin.

"Nurse, please bring Sarah down. Her mother would like to see her."

The nurse ran at the order from the chairman of the asylum. Sarah was dressed beautifully and her hair tied with a yellow bow. She was pleased to see Annie and her aunt and uncle. She brought a folder with paintings she had done and wanted Annie to take one with her.

"It's wonderful, Sarah. You're so clever."

Tea was served and mother and daughter chatted together. Sarah said she wanted to go home with Annie and cried when her mother said that she couldn't.

"I think you should go now, Annie. You're upsetting Sarah and I think it would be advisable if you didn't come for a while."

"I don't want to stop seeing my daughter, Edward."

"I know you're concerned. But as you can see, she is well cared for and we visit often. She isn't without family."

"I want to know how she's getting along, Edward."

"I can arrange that. Maybe an update every quarter of a year?"

"That would be wonderful."

She relented. She couldn't look after Sarah as they did in the sanatorium. She was fed she was able to paint and draw and she was safe.

"Unfortunately, we are not going your way to town. But please allow me to give you a shilling for the omnibus." Edward gave her two shillings. She didn't want to take it but she did.

"Thank you, Edward .You're most generous."

From the corner of her eye she could see Lucille smiling. Edward and his wife would be able to dine out on the story for years. When she got back to town, Annie bought a plate of meat and potato pie and a jug of gravy. She ate her fill and wondered what Edward and Lucille would be having for their supper.

Annie was in need of company so went to the tavern and sat with the regulars. They were singing a sad lament and she joined in, happy to be among her own kind that night.

Annie recognised Robert Mann from the mortuary. He was stood with another much taller man. He tried to look superior to the other customers. He had a short driving-stick and tapped it gently on the bar as though it was a gentleman's cane. He was speaking to his companion and watching the women who were mostly drunk on the ale or gin that flowed through the tavern. He recognised Annie and gave her a quick nod of the head. She could feel his eyes following her as she moved around the bar. He broke the silence and tried to chat with her when she worked at the top end of the bar. His teeth were broken, and she could smell onions on his breath. He was with the other assistant who was tall and thin. There was no reaction from him. All he did was stare into his ale. They were an unlikely couple, but were joined at the hip. Money didn't seem to be a problem for the two men. They drank their fill and bought other customers beer. Robert Mann fancied his chances with Annie and, as his confidence grew, he attempted to compliment Annie on her hair or the way she was dressed. He bought her drinks throughout the night. She was aware that at some time or other she would be expected to repay him.

Chapter Thirty
Friday 24th February, 1888

Annie went to work on the Friday night of the 24th February. It was a slow evening. There was a transient trade with groups of soldiers and sailors having a few drinks and then moving on. At the end of the bar Robert Mann stood with his silent companion.

"Now then, Annie. You look a fine woman tonight. Red suits you." He was referring to the satin red ribbon that tied in her unruly hair.

"Thank you, sir."

She smiled at him. "Please, it's Robert. And my friend here is James. We both work at the mortuary."

"A very special employment, Robert. You hold an important place in the community."

Annie could see Robert Mann puff out his chest even further. James Hatfield had seen into her mind and recognised she was being sarcastic. He looked at her with dead grey eyes. Annie shivered as though someone had walked over her grave.

"You're right, Annie. We're custodians of the unliving."

He pushed his glass forward to replenish his ale. James Hatfield followed suit.

"You must have a drink with us, Annie. A schooner of port?"

She thanked him and took the money. Each time he

ordered a drink he bought Annie one until she felt a little drunk.

"How about a bite of supper after you have finished?" asked Robert.

She didn't want to get involved but felt obliged.

"Just a quick bite then. I'm a little tired. It'll be a long day tomorrow." She wasn't lying. She had to start at twelve noon and would finish at twelve at night.

"Of course, my dear."

He nudged his friend who drank his beer and left.

After a supper of sausages and potatoes they walked down St George's Court to find a dark corner. The drink had deadened Annie's mind. It was so clinical these days - petticoat skirts up and let them get on with it. Robert Mann was no different to any other. It was over and done with in a breath. He had given her sixpence and she waved goodbye.

That night she dreamt of Sarah and Richard and the times they all walked in the park on a Sunday and listened to the band. She strained her ears trying to hear the music in her head but all that was there was the sound of screaming from some poor soul who was being beaten, dogs yapping and a group of drunks singing a popular music hall song. The screaming went on and on until she jumped and realised it was her own voice that the painful sound was coming from.

She didn't rise until eleven o'clock. London was bustling but it was an effort to raise her body from the bed. She drank a little rice milk and washed, capturing her hair under a blue ribbon. Maybe this would be a lucky day finding a shilling in the road.

Chapter Thirty-One
Saturday 25th February, 1888

The tavern was spilling at the seams. There had been two great ships in nearby St George's docks. Men pushed and shoved at the bar, elbowing their neighbour to catch the barmaid's eye.

"Here, Annie. Here."

She was quick on her feet and without much delay served the customers. Robert Mann was with his companion James Hatfield. The mortuary assistant had an air of smugness among his fellow drinking buddies. He whispered to James Hatfield, the receiver showing a set of brown stained teeth. It wasn't as much smile as it was a grimace. The hair on the back of Annie's neck stood on end.

"Hey, sweetheart. Let's have some ale here." A tall dark-haired soldier had pushed his way to the front of the bar.

"Three large ales and a glass of gin for yourself." Annie smiled back at him.

"You've a lovely smile. What's your name?"

"It's Annie."

"Annie, I will die for you. How about sharing a glass or two with me after you've finished?"

"Maybe." She tried to act a little coy.

"Come on. You know you like me." He had a broad beam of a smile.

"Maybe," she said and laughed.

At the other end of the bar, Robert Mann wasn't looking so pleased. He had watched the exchange between the soldier and Annie, and he didn't like it. He thought he had bought a stake in her. She could see him grumbling to James Hatfield, watching her every move. It was half past midnight when Annie finished, there were still a few ardent drinkers in the bar, but the landlord said he could manage. Outside the tavern, the young soldier called to her. He held a half bottle of gin. She laughed at him then saw Robert Mann. He had also been waiting for her. She walked over to the soldier who put his arms around her and kissed her on the cheek. Robert Mann's face was bright red with fury. He hit his driving stick hard to the wall. Annie wasn't having it. She didn't belong to anyone anymore. She was a free spirit.

Annie had a wonderful happy couple of hours. They sang to the barrel organ, they drank in another tavern and ate crispy pork rind. Of course she had to do her business, but that was fun as well. They were both too drunk to perform.

"Annie my sweet, I have to go. But you were wonderful my love."

He kissed her again and left.

She was still in the alley when, from out of the dark shadows, two men appeared.

"Who is it? Leave me be."

She was frightened. The two men moved forward and she could see who it was.

"Robert, you frightened me. What are you doing?"

"Free with your wares aren't you, Annie? You don't keep it fresh for your regulars, do you?" He turned to James Hatfield. "She's just a whore like all the rest, James. Just like you said."

"Stop it, Robert. You're frightening me."

"It's Mr Mann to you."

The taller of the men grabbed Annie from the back. He pushed her to the floor and held her as Robert Mann flung her petticoats above her head. She tried to struggle and scream but it was useless, the two men were bigger than her and stronger. Robert Mann pushed his body into hers for a moment then she felt a blunt object penetrate her vagina. The pain ran through her body. She tried to scream but her petticoat had been stuffed into her mouth. There was more movement and the men changed positions.

She felt cold steel to her stomach. She was to be murdered. She was going to fight to the end and could hear the snorting from the monster that was assaulting her.

"Hey what's going on?" she heard someone shout.

The petticoat was taken from her mouth, but it was replaced by a hand that smelt of carbolic soap.

"Now then, lady. You have a reprieve. But let me tell you if you tell anyone we will come for you. Remember we know where you live and where you work. There's also that girl of yours in the asylum. Say one word and we'll come for you. Are you clear?"

Annie nodded and laid in her own blood as the two ran away.

"Who's there?" The shout was given again. A young policeman held his lamp up to look into the dark corners of the alley. He saw a pile of rags close to the wall and heard the sound of an injured animal. Annie raised her hand.

"Please sir, help me." The policeman was horrified at the sight of Annie.

Her face was bloody and her petticoats disarrayed but soaked in dark red blood. Annie lost consciousness.

Chapter Thirty-Two

She awoke in a bed with clean sheets. She was in a ward with six other patients, a doctor and a nurse standing beside her. She was in terrible pain.

"Oh god, please help me."

"What's your name, ma'am? What's happened to you?"

"Annie Millwood. I live in Star Place."

"Who has done this to you?"

She shook her head. She couldn't say she was too frightened.

"I was walking home from the tavern. It's where I work. A man accosted me. I think he stabbed me."

"He stabbed you many times. What did he look like?"

Annie mumbled that he was tall and dark, then lost consciousness.

A policeman called at the Whitechapel infirmary to take details of the incident. It was thought she had been attacked by a customer. It was a regular occurrence although this had been an exceptionally vicious one. Annie made slow progress, but she was too frightened to return to her lodgings. Angus the landlord of the tavern had heard that she was in the infirmary and soon after arrived with a bag of apples.

"How are you Annie? Who was it? Tell me. I'll make sure he doesn't do it again. It wasn't that young soldier you were with, was it?"

"No, Angus. He was a good boy. We just had a bit of fun, that's all."

She didn't want to tell him she was having sex with the customers but needn't have worried. Angus knew just what his girls were doing, but it was hard in the area, and needs must.

"Your landlady called in the tavern. She thought you had done a moonlight flit. I told her about what had happened. She said she couldn't save your room."

Annie cried. Being homeless was the last thing she needed.

In three weeks, she was strong enough to be released. The infirmary managed to secure a place at South Grove workhouse Mile End Road. She was grateful she had a place to go but dreaded the workhouse. On Monday the twenty-first of March she went to the workhouse. She had new petticoats bought from the pawn shop and paid from charitable funds. She had a blue skirt and blue blouse, a pair of stockings and a new second-hand pair of boots. One of the nurses had brought her a knitted shawl. She felt clean and cared for. The workhouse at South Grove smelled of disinfectant and dirty bodies. Annie was on a ward with fifty other women. She was given a nightdress and a small piece of cloth to clean herself with. The food was poor with vegetables boiled beyond belief and, of course, gruel. The bread was always days old, what did they do with the fresh bread? She had to pick oakum in a morning and in the afternoon to pay for her keep. Annie was in tremendous pain, but she was still on the rota for scrubbing the dining tables.

Saturday 31st March, 1888

Three weeks had passed, and Annie was struggling to complete her duties. She wanted to regain some strength so she could return to the tavern. She had picked oakum in the morning and, having finished a sack full, dragged it downstairs to the horse and cart waiting for its load. She was dazed by the bright sunlight in the street. Annie then saw her worst nightmare. Robert Mann and James Hatfield were stood talking to the cart driver.

"Well look who we have here. It's Annie. What are you doing?"

The two men surrounded her.

"Annie has come down in the world a little. What do you think, James?"

"I think you're right, Mr Mann, as always."

"I don't suppose you've the time for a couple of customers Annie? Both fine gentlemen."

"No, Robert. No, I can't."

"What do you mean you can't? Fetch her, James." James Hatfield looked up and down the road. He put his arm around Annie's neck, and they took her down the passage into the back yard of the workhouse. Annie couldn't scream. Her heart was beating too fast and her throat felt constricted. Robert Mann lifted her skirts.

"Robert."

James Hatfield felt the body of Annie crumble in his arms. He let her drop to the floor.

"Bloody hell, James. Did you have to squeeze her throat so tight?"

"No, she just went."

Robert Mann felt for a pulse. They knew about dead bodies and Annie's was certainly dead. The two men crept from the backyard and went to the mortuary cart and rode away.

***

Inquest for Annie Millwood, 5th April 1888.
Coroner: Wynne Baxter.
Report: Sudden effusion into the pericardium from the rupture of the left pulmonary artery through ulceration.
Conclusion: The death was from natural causes unrelated to her vicious attack over a month before.

Martha Tabram

Chapter Thirty-Three

I can't move. The lanky one has my arms. The other one has a fancy driving stick. He's pulling it apart. A flash of steel in the gas light hurt my eyes. I see a carousel with horses. My life in pictures. I must be dead. I came into the world on the 10th May 1849 at 17 Marshall Street, Southwark, London. I wasn't born with a silver spoon in my mouth, I was born to work, to scramble for food, heat and light. I never knew anything different as all the families in the neighbouring streets and terraces close by were the same. My earliest memories were those of my elder brothers and sisters telling me to be quiet, or putting their dirty hands over my mouth, so as not to attract my father, who was laying into my mother with his leather belt. The shouting and beatings would frighten me, because if my father heard a sound from us, he would take the stairs two at a time with his leather belt already out of his pants swinging it above his head. It was usually Stephan that got the leather most of the time, but that was because he would stand in front of us girls.

At sixteen my brother Henry left home. He'd gone because he couldn't stand the arguing and the increase in mother's drinking. My father was Charles White, a hardworking man, but he didn't have much to do with us as children. I respected him but was also frightened of him. My mother, Elisabeth, was the opposite. I don't know how they got together in the first place. Mother was quick witted but lazy. She would sit at the kitchen table and demand jobs done.

"Martha, bring the washing in. Mary Ann, go scrub the step. Stephan, stoke the fire. Esther, sew a button on your father's Sunday shirt."

We would all say yes mother, because if mother got angry all hell would have to pay. I remember her complaining about how little housekeeping father gave her, and how she had to cut currants in half to survive the week.

It was much easier when my sister Esther left to become a parlour maid in a big house in Pall Mall. My sister Mary Ann who was three years older than me was left to our own devices. Mother was fun. She often drank during the day. We would go to the markets and she would steal apples from the barrows that lined the street. We would wait on the steps of the White Hart Inn on Whitechapel Road, while she had a little chat to her friends, taking in a glass or two of gin. I loved the smell of the tobacco, porter and the perfume of the gin. If she had a couple we would sneak inside, and she would offer the glass to me for a taste. Mary Ann never liked the liquor, so I would get her mouthful. Mother seemed proud that I could stand up after a few snorts of the brew.

"Well she has got good taste like her mother. Come on my little darlings, let's go home to that miserable old sod of a husband."

We would sing music hall songs all the way home. When we got back to our house, father would be sat in his chair. We would run upstairs to get out of the way of the inevitable screaming and shouting. Every Saturday night, mother would have a wash and apply powder and rouge to her drink-worn face. Father came home with his pay packet. I would clean his boots for a farthing and Mary Ann would brush his coat for hers. My mother held her hand out for her housekeeping. There was always an argument, my mother saying it wasn't enough.

"How do you expect me to run a house on this? These children are almost starving."

I always thought we were. The hunger caused pains in my stomach, made worse if my mother had been out a few days during the week. Food was never on her shopping list. We would scrape the dripping bowl with crusts of bread and supplement our diet with what we could steal from the markets. But Saturdays were different. The excitement used to run through the house. Even mother had her ritual that had to be played every week. The arguing would last until eight o'clock then mother would get her bonnet and we were told to go to bed. They would walk arm in arm like star crossed lovers. Mary Ann and I used to give them a couple of minutes then follow hiding under the shadows. We would giggle, pushing each other over. It was children playing, and life was harsh.

My parents usually went to the White Hart Inn, and this night was no different. I licked my finger and made a neat circle on the grimy window and put my eye up close. My mother and father were sat with a group of other drinkers. Father had his glass of ale and mother a glass of porter.

"Martha, lets go in now," said Mary Ann.

"No not yet. They haven't had enough. Let them have another."

Mary Ann was so impatient. We waited another ten minutes then presented ourselves by the sides of our parents.

"What the bloody hell are you doing here?"

Father was never pleased to see us.

"Aww the little darlings. My little girls, Charlie, give em a penny."

She shoved my father. He begrudgingly gave us the money, holding the penny out. I made a grab for it and we ran all the way to the sweetshop.

Mrs Drake had the best of all shops. There were boxes of fancy chocolates tied with ribbons and jars of boiled sweets, all the colours of the rainbow, fruit jellies and sticks of woody liquorice root. We bought bullseyes and sherbet lemons, carefully sharing our cache and cracking them into two if there was more on one pile than the other. We laid in bed and told stories, knowing that in an hour or two our peace would be broken by mother and father arriving home.

Chapter Thirty-Four
1865

I don't think my mother was afraid of my father. She always stood up to him. She would wear her black eyes like medals. She would visit the neighbours to tell them what he had done. We didn't have many possessions and those we did have would have been smashed over my father's head - the brown teapot, complete with tea, Aunt Peggy's beautiful butterfly vase smashed into a dozen pieces. I tried to stick it together with flour and water, but it was beyond repair. The arguments were also an excuse for my mother to leave the house, slamming the door behind her and going to the tavern. We were then left without supper and had to find scraps, or father would send us to the hot potato man, for potatoes in their jackets wrapped in newspaper.

Mary Ann left home when she got pregnant by her boyfriend Alfred. He had a decent job at the sugar refinery, and they moved into two rooms near Brick Lane. I was left to put up with mother's tantrums and father's arguments. She still got the same housekeeping and I was the only child at home. I had a job on a flower stall at Spitalfields market. The money was fair, and I wasn't in the house with mother all day. The problem with mother's drinking got to be very difficult to handle.

One day father said he had enough. He took his Sunday jacket and his collars in the wooden box and left. Mother shouted abuse at him as he walked down the street. I'd begged him to stay as he was in the kitchen. He said he couldn't do it anymore. He was so calm. I watched from behind the curtains as his proud body marched off and my mother's great hips swayed as she shouted abuse and shook the fat on her arms. I think my mother's action of staying out all night on one of her marathon drinking sessions didn't help, then father calling her a tart then she hits him with the sweeping brush. That was that. He left half a crown on the kitchen table and walked out. The neighbours stood on their doorsteps laughing at the spectacle.

After father left, mother shouted and screamed for two days until she eventually calmed down. It was up to me then to be the breadwinner.

"It's a good job you're bringing in some money or we would have been high and dry."

I felt the weight of the world on my shoulders, but it became calm in the house and laughter returned. The Saturday ritual was now that my mother met me from work at night to take my wages from me, leaving me with a shilling for the week. We went together to The Britannia Tavern and joined the rabble fighting for room at the bar to enjoy a glass or two of gin. I was approached by a young sailor one evening and he whispered in my ear.

"Hello, darling. Why don't you leave your old friend and come and earn a couple of bob around the corner?"

I knew what he meant. You couldn't live in that part of London without knowing about the birds and the bees. I'd lifted my skirts for a boy before. That was when I believed in love and fairy tales. But I was sixteen and now I was a woman. And money was money.

"Let's see it first."

He pushed a florin across the table. I picked it up and put it in the inside pocket of my corset, close to my breast.

"Come on them."

I took his hand and we went out of the back door of the inn. We found ourselves a quiet spot and I lifted my petticoat while he pushed himself into me. After a few thrusts it was over and two bob was earned. So we were all happy. I had money in my pocket, my mother had my wages, and the jolly Jack tar had relieved his itch.

Chapter Thirty-Five

One Friday night a few years later I called at the tavern after work. My mother met me at the bar. We had a couple of glasses of gin and a smart man with a good moustache came to sit with us. He told funny tales that I found most amusing. His boots were shining just as father's used to be. Mother came close to my ear.

"He's got a bob or two. Look at his boots."

She could have been reading my mind. He introduced himself as Henry Tabram. He was a foreman packer.

"And are you married, Mr Tabram?" I asked saucily.

"Not yet Miss White. Not yet." His smile twinkled and he captured my heart with the thought of a man with a regular source of income.

"I was wondering, Miss White, if you would accompany me to the music hall tomorrow with your mother of course."

"She will. I haven't been there for years," my mother butted in.

I was eager to go, but wasn't too keen on mother being my chaperon. Not that I needed one.

"That is most kind, sir. Please call me Martha."

We met and had a wonderful time, in spite of my mother. He was a pleasant man, but he didn't set fire to my fire. Mother said that it wasn't about love, it is about who could look after you.

***

Mother was angry when I said I was planning to leave and to move in with Henry on Pleasant Street. She said she would have to find a room in a lodging house because she couldn't afford the rent by herself. Henry's place was comfortable with curtains to the windows and a full tea set with tea pot. I still worked at the market, but Henry didn't want me to. Saturdays were the same with mother wanting some of my wages and I looked forward to taking a few glasses with Henry, although he wasn't a big drinker.

He would tap his pocket watch, then looked at the mantle clock.

"Where have you been until this time?"

"You're not my lord and master, Henry Tabram. Nor my husband," I shouted back, realising I sounded just like my mother those years before.

"Well we shall have to change that."

I turned around and he was down on one knee.

"Will you marry me, Martha?"

"Yes, I will." It was somebody else's voice that answered him.

We got married on the 25th December 1869. Mother and Mary Ann attended after church and we all went to The Britannia Inn and had mulled wine and pie. Mother said that I had done well for myself. Henry then said that I should finish work and look after him and the children that were bound to come along. Finishing work was wonderful, no more early mornings, no rose thorns stuck in my fingers. I cooked and cleaned and became the housewife Henry wanted me to be.

My first child Henry was born in 1871 then soon after in 1872 John came along. It was hard looking after two small boys and I wasn't appreciated. Henry would come home from work, have his supper, then sit by the fire all evening smoking his pipe. I felt cheated. There was London out there with all its treats and treasures, the freak shows and the penny dreadfuls. There was always a jug of ale in the pantry as nobody drank the water unless you wanted typhoid. But ale wasn't enough, it was the feeling I got from the gin or rum, the perfume and aroma went deep inside of me, and the world was a better place. When you are in drink you aren't hungry, you don't need a new bonnet, you don't care if someone is in a carriage or you are walking. The men you are with look the same and you don't worry about the time they take to be satisfied. It's just another penny in the pot. I often went to meet my mother or sisters in the tavern, leaving Henry to look after his two boys, if he didn't want to come with me that was his own fault.

"Don't be late back, Martha." His face looked like a prune.

"Yes, dearie," I'd say, a dutiful wife. But I couldn't wait to get out of the bloody house. An hour later I would have had half a bottle of gin and a cosy cuddle with a soldier boy.

"Be careful, Martha. Henry might be like your father and leave. Then what would you do?" Esther was always the sensible sister. I really should have taken heed. Henry did try to cut my drinking down by not giving me money. Unfortunately, it just gave me an opportunity to expand my business. Having sex in a dark alley enabled me to drink almost every day. I'd passed out a few times and then gone to the clinic at the London Hospital. The doctor told me it was the gin and that I should abstain for my children's sake. Henry attempted to stop me drinking in a different way. He would be at the front door with his belt off, ready to beat me. However, I am my mother's daughter and always take it like a trojan. Strange that when you're in drink you feel numb. You feel the first blow then everyone after that is just as a ripple across water.

Chapter Thirty-Six

1875

Henry said that he had his fill of me falling over.

"Well who's going to feed your children and provide them with shelter?"

"Find some drunk in the tavern. I'm sure someone will step forward."

And he left, just as my father did. I ran to the door and shouted at him. He didn't even look back. I was my mother all over again. There was no money coming in, so I had to sell my only asset on a regular basis, but the money wasn't enough. Then a neighbour, Mrs Kipper, said that as I was legally married to Henry, I could get him arrested for desertion. I waited until he came out of work, he looked so smart, hair greased down moustaches neat and boots as though they had never been worn. I was going to enjoy this.

"Well here he is, the man who deserted his wife and children. What are you going to do about it, Henry Tabram?"

He ignored me and walked on.

"Your two boys went to bed hungry last night. What did you have for your supper?"

He still didn't answer me. There was a small crowd gathering.

"I'm going to the police."

I knew that would hurt him more than anything. So I went to the police station with my marriage certificate and they went and arrested him, much to his surprise. He talked himself out of the situation with a promise, that he would resolve the problem with a weekly allowance of twelve shillings a week. That would be enough to pay the rent and for food. I was happy enough with that, and I could earn a little extra from getting a customer to pay for my drink.

Chapter Thirty-Seven
1876

Henry Turner wasn't my cup of tea. He was slovenly, with dirt in his fingernails. He was a carpenter in 1876 but he didn't have his own tools. I should have known he was no good then, a real craftsman, always had his own tools.

He sat just a little too close to me then clinked his glass onto mine.

"Hello, my dear."

"I'm not your dear," I said.

"Would you be my dear if I bought you a couple of glasses of this delightful porter?"

"I might be."

A girl has to make a crust, I thought. We ended up in the back yard of the inn with my skirts up and his trousers around his ankles. He was more drunk than I was.

"Ere, mind where you're putting that."

He had more than his two pennies worth but still wanted more, so I suggested he come home with me. He bought hot sausages and we rolled along. The boys were fast asleep, and we enjoyed a steamy session on the kitchen floor.

"You've had your money's worth."

The cheeky bugger tried to mount me again.

"Martha, you're my kind of woman."

"Yes, they all say that." I was good at bringing a smile to the face of many a man.

"You need to be off before my boys are up."

"I need to find somewhere to live. The lodging house has closed. You don't know of a place?"

I didn't believe him for a moment. But it was good to have a bit of company. After Henry left it was a bit quiet with just the two lads.

"You can stay, but you need to be out of the way on a Saturday when my husband comes around with my housekeeping."

"Of course, Martha." I did like his smile.

Saturday was pay day. Henry would walk straight into my kitchen at six-thirty. He would sit at the table and count twelve shilling in two-shilling pieces. Then I'd get a lecture on how to spend it, the rent, the food. I nodded until he finished. He would then comment on the state of the house, it was untidy, or the floor needed sweeping. He took ten minutes to look around then left. I would go to the tavern with Mr Turner, but Henry Turner couldn't keep up with me. He hated it when he had to go home and leave me making merry, especially if I had a soldier on my arm plying me with all my drinks, and a promise of a bob or two.

"You're a harlot, Martha Tabram," he would shout when I eventually got home.

"I most certainly am," I would answer.

Chapter Thirty-Eight

1879

Henry Turner was with me for almost three years until Henry Tabram found out about my living arrangements.

"Don't think you're going to get a penny piece out of me, Martha Tabram."

Funny how people use your full name when they want to be angry with you. Poor Henry. He was angry. The ends of his nostrils flared out as he spoke. I suppose he felt humiliated, but why should I care? It was difficult from then on. I couldn't pay the rent. Mr Turner wasn't the master carpenter he claimed to be and lost his job. We were both hard up. I tried to waylay my husband from work, to make him feel guilty or embarrass him. It wasn't until I took Henry and John with me that he gave me two shillings and said he would give me that every week for the boys.

1881

Things didn't get any better with Henry Turner. He didn't like the idea of paying money into the pot. One day I got up and he'd gone without a kiss my arse or a goodbye. The landlord was asking for his money, but we didn't have anything to give him.

"Mrs Tabram, open the door."

He rattled the doorknob.

"Shall I open the door, mama?"

"No, Henry. Come here."

I sat behind the door and put my finger to my lips. The door moved and we were pushed to one side.

"Come on, you're nearly four weeks behind with your rent. Get your stuff."

We were thrown out onto the street without ceremony. The boys were crying. A policeman on duty asked what the matter was, and I had told him we had just been evicted. He took us to the casual ward at Old Montague Street workhouse. I could smell the carbolic soap before we got inside the ward. There must have been sixty cots, like boxes, end to end. The boys were expected to sleep with me. The tiled walls made the room feel cold. We were with the scum of the earth. The three of us slept together in the bed with a blanket stretched over us. We slept in our clothes, just in case someone would come along and steal what we were laid in. At eight o'clock in the morning we were woken by a bell ringing loud enough to wake the dead. A long line of women and children began forming, we hoped, for food. John said he was hungry. The queue moved slowly, and I could see the front of it as it snaked into the dining room. Each person was handed a slice of bread by an inmate. We then sat down to an empty place where a bowl of grey gruel sat cold. The boys ate theirs greedily. I couldn't stomach the mess in the bowl and shared it between my sons.

"Mama, are we going to live here?" asked Henry.

"Not bloody likely. Maybe just another night I think."

I needed to get somewhere for us to stay. We were shut out of the ward with the matron telling us that we could return at five o'clock. The old woman at the side of us said because it was Tuesday it would be vegetable soup for supper. I went to my mother who said that she couldn't have us. She wasn't well, and the boys would tip her over the edge. It was useless going to any of my siblings, they were all too good for me now.

As I walked down Brick Lane I saw Henry Turner. He started to cross the street away from me.

"Don't you turn your back on me, Henry Turner. You've left us in the lurch and straight to the workhouse." I cried, ranted and raved.

He didn't look too good either, so we agreed to search for lodgings and to support each other. He'd sold some trinkets that morning, so we had a few shillings to rent a room in a lodging house at Star Place Commercial Road.

There was a bed and set of drawers. It wasn't very comfortable, but it was a hundred times better than the workhouse. Mrs Bousfield, who owned the lodging house, gave us two old blankets. She said that she felt sorry for the boys. I didn't really like the idea of sharing a bed again with Henry. I had to deal with wandering hands in the tavern but to get home and have my sleep interrupted was something else. The only way to feel better was to have an extra gin or two.

Our arrangement went on well for a month or two. It was still a struggle to pay the rent. Mrs Bousfield always had her supper at six o'clock. This was the ideal time to leave, clicking the door quietly, so she didn't hear. I didn't have a pimp and wasn't part of some organised gang that operated in London. I think I was too old for them. I started late and then became married. Having Henry Turner about served that purpose, to look out for you. Henry always wanted his fair share of the act. It just meant I needed to do twice as much.

Chapter Thirty-Nine

May 1888

I met my friend Mary Ann Connolly in about May of the year 1888. She was in the tavern with a soldier and we got talking. Her nickname was Pearly Poll. She was as bright as a button, just how I used to be before age and poverty had caught up with me. Her golden curls cascaded down from her bonnet. We were a great couple. Anyone in our company had a good time.

"Here, there are two fine women. Draw a chair and have a glass."

The two soldiers moved chairs, so we could fit onto their table.

"What will it be, ladies?"

We both laughed. That was the last thing we were. They didn't want ladies, they wanted whores, and that was just what we were. I could see Henry Turner sat in the corner. He was there to count my customers. He had a tankard of ale in front of him and he would be wanting more. You had to have a couple of drinks from your customers before you lifted your skirts otherwise the few pennies you received wouldn't have been enough. Then you had to be as quick as you could to make sure you got another likely lad. I did all-nighters but only to regular customers. Henry didn't like me staying out all night as he thought he might be left with paying the rent.

We had to leave Star Street during the night. We were a few weeks behind in rent. I went to stay with Poll for a short time. I didn't know or care where Henry went. He'd given me one too many black eyes and was lazy. But I didn't need a man to look after me. I'd lived on the streets of London for long enough to know you had to look after yourself in this world. I still loved the smell of the tavern after all these years, the noise of the rowdy customers, the tobacco which stung your nostrils and the characters that hid in the dark corners. I was free of the boys, one was now a soldier, the other an apprentice. They didn't speak to me in the street. Their father had turned them against me long ago. At least I didn't have to look after them anymore.

Chapter Forty

July 1888

It was a hot summer and the streets were full of flies living on the human waste that was piled in the gutters. I'd slept in a doorway for two nights and my bones ached. I met with Pearly Poll and we talked a couple of sailors into buying us a few glasses. We took turns going into the backyard to pay for our gin. I'd used my wiping cloth half a dozen times that night. I secreted it away in my petticoats then returned to my drink and the merriment of the crowd. A man at the bar raised his hat to me. He was dressed quite smart for that area - a navy dress coat that bore the symbol of the workhouse. I think he must have been one of the custodians. He was surveying our group with a sneer on his face. He obviously didn't approve of us having a drink or two. He held a silver-topped driving stick, too short to be a cane, in his left hand. The man at the side of him was much taller. They were both older than me, trying to look like a couple of gents, but falling far from it. I felt a shiver through my body.

"Has someone walked across your grave, Martha?"

"Yes, Henry Tabram dancing on it."

They all laughed. Poll moved over and spoke into my ear.

"Them two at the bar are the ones that's giving you the shivers. They're from the workhouse mortuary."

I looked at them both then caught the smell of carbolic soap.

"I think we have a couple of dead bodies up at the bar,

girls."

I laughed out loud and the other girls joining me.

Robert Mann came to the side of the table and struck it with his stick, causing the glasses to fall over.

"Shut your mouths. You're nothing but a handful of tarts. You'll be sorry, trust me."

They left by the side door.

Chapter Forty-One

Saturday 4th August, 1888

I was destitute. I'd spent Friday night outside the chandlers on Brick Lane. I had been lucky the weather had been fair, but I needed to get somewhere before the autumn came. I hadn't a farthing. Then I saw Henry Turner. He looked in the same situation I was in, but he never was a snappy dresser.

"Henry my love, please help me. You must have a shilling or two to spare. I haven't had a morsel of bread all day."

He tried to walk away.

"Please, Henry."

He must have felt something for me as he dug down into his waistcoat pocket and gave me a shilling and sixpence.

"Go to Commercial Street, Martha, to the warehouse, and buy some hair combs. You can easily double your money by selling them on."

He always had big ideas, not that they ever worked. I bought a penny loaf and ate it quickly, giving me a belly ache. I called at the Ten Bells and Poll was there already. I told her I only had five-pence to my name, so we had a couple of glasses of gin. The evening perked up and I managed a couple of knee trembles, so we could put a few more glasses on the table. The next couple of nights I spent in a cheap lodging house, the bed jumping with wildlife and still warm when I got in. My poor old kidneys ached from the gin, but at least I could sleep without one eye open.

Bank Holiday Monday, 6th August, 1888

It was Bank Holiday Monday, and everyone was in great merriment. There were fire-eaters and acrobats playing to large audiences on the streets. I tried to take a wallet from one of the toffs, but he turned around and told me to be on my way or he would get the coppers. The Ten Bells was full in the early afternoon. The landlord had placed plates of pork pie and pickled onions on each of the tables. It was a feast. Me and Poll got all the girls singing and a couple of soldiers joined us. One was a Corporal and the other a Private. They were having a grand time. Poll suggested we all go to another hostelry in Whitechapel High Street. They both agreed as we had come to a business agreement for the night.

I did have a merry time. It was after eleven when we walked out of the inn. I walked towards St George's Yard with my lad, Poll was taking hers to Angel Arch. It was a bit too dark for me. St George's Yard and buildings was a safer spot. The tenements above ensured that people were close by, and I do try to be in calling distance. In the yard I found a windowsill to park my bum on and lifted my skirts. The young lad wasn't that well-endowed, so I had to shuffle around a bit. It was soon over and done with. He tripped when pulling his trousers up and I laughed. He had no sense of humour and went off cursing me. It was a good job I got my money first, I thought. I may even have time to pick up another unsuspecting young or old man.

"Have you got time, dearie?"

It made me jump. The man stood in the shadow. He had very few teeth in his gappy smile.

"Have you got the money, sweetheart?"

I straightened my skirts.

"How about half a crown and come up to my rooms. I live here at number forty-five. We can have a little drink. I bet you like a gin or two."

Now that is what I call luck and this old fella wouldn't take much rocking. I reached the first landing and we were joined by another. He pulled his driver's stick apart, then I heard a pop in my ears as the blade found its way to my heart. There was a faint smell of carbolic soap.

***

Inquest for Martha Tabram, 23rd August 1888
Died: August 7th, 1888.
Coroner: Deputy Coroner George Collier.
Inquest: The Working Lads' Institute, Whitechapel Road.
Conclusion: Murder by person or persons unknown.

Rose Mylett

Chapter Forty-Two

Catherine was a beautiful child, blond hair and a fair complexion. Her mother would comb and dress her hair to attract customers to her flower basket at the edge of Spitalfields market. Little Rose, as she became known, grew up entertaining the great unwashed of London. The little girl enjoyed the attention of the crowd. People would stand around and watch her sing and dance by her mother's flower basket. The crowd would throw farthings into her mother's bonnet which sat on the cobbles. The family struggled, as many did in Victorian England. They lived in two rooms of a large terraced house. The backyard had a block of four privies which were used by over forty people. Meals were cooked in a large black frying pan set upon the open grate or food was bought from the many food stalls that lined the streets. By twelve, Rose no longer danced for an audience, she had to work to help support the family. Her father had bought her a large basket from his meagre wages in a warehouse. This was filled most days with fresh roses. Her pitch was on the opposite corner of the street to her mother, who would take careful notice of the sales. She had to ensure her daughter didn't short change her. Rose matured into a beautiful girl and there were many young men, and older ones for that matter, she caught the eye of. Not many chanced their arm with a mother sat looking on. Mrs Mylett would shout profanities at anyone taking longer than two minutes with her daughter.

"Get your bleeding eyes off her. It's the flowers for sale,

not her."

Rose would feel embarrassment at her mother's outbursts, but she knew she was only protecting her from unwanted advances. That was until Patrick Smith came onto the scene.

Chapter Forty-Three

Patrick Smith was a young man who had decided some time ago that he wasn't going to live in poverty. He'd run away from Ireland after murdering his violent father. Patrick had caught a boat and ended up in London, first becoming a lawful individual holding down a very good job as a bookkeeper. His life was changed when he stole money from his master. It had been hard keeping a step-in front of the police and to earn a living. He'd hidden among the slums of Whitechapel among all the thieves and vagabonds of old London Town.

He stole, he beat men and women for landlords who had not got their rent. He smuggled the best brandy from rowing boats on the Thames in the dead of the night. He enjoyed being known as a hard man. He had a dozen young boys who would do little jobs for him, ensuring they took the risks while he pocketed the rewards. He had lodgings in a terraced house near George's Yard. It was like most houses in the area, dilapidated, holes in the roof and a staircase you could only walk up one side. The young lads hung out there and Patrick had his own bedroom. The kitchen was always busy with two girls cooking sausages and onions for those that wanted to eat. Patrick thought that if he looked after his gang, they would be loyal to him.

He first caught sight of Rose on a Friday morning. He didn't usually go to Spitalfields Market, but he was meeting up with another entrepreneur when he heard the sweet sound of Rose's call.

"Come along, gents. Roses for your love. Open your heart to a loved one."

Patrick stood on the opposite corner watching the blond girl.

"She's fine isn't she?"

Patrick looked down at the old woman sat on the cobbles. She had a basket of cornflowers.

"She is that," he said with his Irish brogue.

"Give me a bunch of your flowers, Mrs."

He bent down and took the flowers from her, offering a half penny in exchange.

"She's mine that one, my girl."

"She's your daughter?"

"My beautiful Rose."

He tried to see some resemblance but there wasn't any. A life of drink and a poor diet had dissolved any beauty the old hag had ever had. He crossed the street and tipped his hat to Rose, offering her the bunch of cornflowers that echoed the colour of her eyes.

"For you, young Miss. Patrick Smith at your disposal."

Rose flushed her cheeks and turned crimson. She looked across at her mother who was smiling. She accepted and curtsied.

"Catherine Mylett. But people call me Rose."

Chapter Forty-Four

Patrick felt lucky. He sweet-talked his way into Rose's life. He'd bought the basket of flowers from her and then took the roses and gave them to her astonished mother.

"I'm taking your daughter to the pie shop for a bite to eat. We won't be going anywhere else, missus. I promise. And I'll deliver her back here in one hour."

Mrs Mylett was amused. She remembered when the boys used to flock around her. That was an age ago. Now it was Rose's turn, and this one seemed to have a bit of money. He was true to his word, and an hour later he sauntered back to the corner with Rose smiling sweetly.

"Now then good lady, tomorrow is Saturday. I would like to take Rose and you and your husband to the Music Hall on Commercial Road."

"She's a bit young to be going to the Music Hall, sir. She's barely sixteen."

"There's nothing that would frighten a young lady, I'm sure. Please, my heart will be broken if you deny me."

Rose laughed as he knelt in front of her mother, causing a scene on the cobbles. It was agreed that they would meet at eight o'clock the following evening. He gave Rose sixpence to buy a fancy comb for her hair and a ribbon for her bonnet.

"He didn't kiss you, did he?" her mother questioned.

"No mama of course not. We just had pie, which was delicious. He's very handsome though, isn't he? And so debonair."

"I'll give you that. It's the Irish. They all have the gift of the gab."

Her mother went into a long story about an Irish lad she courted years ago. Rose didn't listen to her though. She was miles away, walking through buttercups, holding the hand of sweet Patrick. Her father wasn't as pleased as her mother but, at least, was happy that someone would pay for a night out. That didn't happen very often. He knew Rose would have a beau soon enough. Better she have someone with some money, because looks don't last for ever. Rose was excited. She had never been to the Music Hall before. The audience was made up of every class, ragged boys at the sides fetching drinks for the mob, whores and their pimps in the gods and sat in the velour seats to the front circle the toffs in evening dress. There was an acrobat, a magician and then a middle-aged woman singing soprano.

"Our Rose could do better than that, Patrick," said her father.

"She surely could, sir. And better to look at." Patrick had the same thought.

"I need to speak to someone. I'll not be long."

The Mylett family enjoyed the girls dancing to a popular melody when Patrick returned with a short round man dressed in tails and a striped waistcoat.

"Ladies and gentlemen, may I introduce to you the owner of this wondrous emporium? Mr George Claypole, sir, Mr and Mrs Mylett, and here is the songbird herself, the beautiful and sweet Rose."

The round man said he was charmed and bowed to everyone. He took hold of Rose's hand and kissed it, making her shiver.

"Please follow me. The curtain will fall in two minutes. I need to speak to you. Please follow." He walked with a shuffle, pushing people out of his way in the corridor. He led them into an office. There were piles of books and empty bottles of gin and porter on a large oak desk.

"Here here."

He threw books from a couple of chairs and Rose and her

mother sat confused at what was happening.

"I hear you can sing ,Miss Rose."

"Only to sell my flowers, sir."

Mr Claypole gestured with his hand.

"Please sing for me."

At first Rose didn't want to, but with encouragement from Patrick and her mother she started to sing a popular tune.

Mr Claypole's face lit up. She did have the voice of an angel and she looked like one too.

"Wonderful You're to be the opening act. What do you say girl? What do you say?"

Rose looked at her mother and father. It would be her dream to sing in the Music Hall.

"How much will she earn?" Her father was blunt and to the point.

"Five shillings a week. How about that?"

The Myletts all stood with their mouths open. It was as much as her father earned.

"She'll do it."

Her mother thought it was a great opportunity. The family would be able to move to better rooms. They would be able to eat well. All for singing sweetly. Mr Claypole gave Patrick ten shillings to buy some clothes that would be suitable for Rose, nothing too fancy or revealing. She would be dressed as someone younger than her sixteen years and would be billed as Sweet Rose.

She would practice the following week and her first night would be next Saturday. Patrick took the family to eat in a dining room on Whitechapel Road where they ate their fill. Patrick arranged to meet Rose and her mother at the market on Monday morning where they picked through second-hand clothes at the pawnbroker's stall. They bought four outfits - a velvet dress coat in green, a blue high-necked dress with a white apron to go over the top, a pink satin dress with white fur around the bottom and a red cape with fur trim. Rose stroked the fur. She'd never had such luxurious things to wear. Patrick felt Rose's excitement and wanted to take hold of her and kiss her, but he knew he had to take things slowly.

This was a sweet girl, unspoilt. He would protect her and wait.

Rose went to the music hall in the afternoon as Mr Claypole had directed her. She felt very nervous but excited. She carried the clothes she had bought. A young boy took the clothes from her and they were put in the dressing room used by the artists. Mr Claypole approved of the purchases and Rose was told to dress in the blue dress and apron. She stood on the stage, her legs shaking. Then the tiny band of musicians struck up a tune and Mr Claypole handed Rose some sheet music.

"You'll have two songs in the first house then two the second. Now the gents that frequent this place want to see a little girl with ribbons like their daughters at home. Innocent and pure." He licked his lips and Rose felt uncomfortable again. Most afternoons, Patrick came to the theatre to watch her and clapped enthusiastically when she finished.

"Your singing is beautiful, Rose." He bent and kissed her hand. She wanted him to sweep her up into his arms and kiss her on the mouth, but she knew he was a gentleman.

On the first Saturday she went to the music hall early. Her mother and father arrived later for the first show. Patrick had a job to do but said he would be there, if a little late. Rose watched from the wings. The hall was bursting with people all drinking and laughing. Her props were set on the stage - a tiny footstool and a doll that she had to cradle in her arms. Her face had been painted by the juggler's wife. It was white like a doll with a cupid bow lip of crimson red. Her hair was dressed in ringlets with two pink ribbons hanging down. She looked like a tiny child of maybe ten years old. Mr Claypole came backstage and told her she looked very pretty. He said that she should sit on the stool and wait for the music to start.

The master of ceremonies, who stood in a box along the stage side, shouted. "And for your pleasure ladies and gentlemen, for the first time in London town, we have Sweet Rose of Tralee."

There was a drum roll and the curtains were pulled back by two ragged boys. The intro to her song started and a tiny sound crept out of Rose's mouth. Mr Claypole was shouting from the wings for her to sing. Rose looked through the crowd and saw Patrick he waved, and she was filled with confidence. She sang her songs to rapturous applause. Rose bowed a dozen times until Mr Claypole had to go on stage and drag her off.

"Well done, my dear. Well done. I liked the nervous start. It gave it truth a little girl lost. Well done I'm most pleased."

Patrick came backstage as she washed the greasepaint off and changed into her normal clothes. Her mother and father congratulated her on her performance although her father didn't like the way she had to wear make-up.

"It's not make-up, father. It's grease paint."

They pushed themselves through the crowds that had gathered in the street outside the hall and went to the local pie shop.

"You were the best act they have ever had on that stage, Rose. You need to be asking for a rise. You're certainly going to have a following after that."

Both her mother and father nodded, agreeing with Patrick's statement. Two soldiers passed them in the street, both singing sweet Rose of Tralee. They all laughed. They walked to the George and went in, Rose had a glass of port, her mother and father a gin and Patrick a glass of ale. The celebration lasted until after midnight. Patrick walked the family home with Rose on his arm at the doorstep of her home. He bent his head and kissed her gently on her cheek. She blushed and quickly ran inside closing the door behind herself.

Chapter Forty-Five

Monday was the only day that Rose didn't work. Her mother wouldn't let her be idle though. She had to be up, as everyone else did, in the house. She walked with her mother to get flowers from the wholesale market. They packed the two large wicker baskets and each carried their load to the corner of the street. Life was busy at any time day or night in that part of London. Hawkers were shouting each other out to get people to trade with them.

"I don't want you getting any airs or graces, Rose. We all have to work, and singing isn't a real job is it? But I'll give you that you put money in the pot."

Rose didn't answer her mother back. That wasn't a wise thing to do. She had tried once and was beaten to within an inch of her life.

"And I'll tell you something else. Although I like Patrick, you need to watch he doesn't take liberties. You know what I mean?"

Rose did know what her mother meant. How could she not? Nearly every woman in the district was having sex down a dark alley. It had become a way of life. She didn't understand what actually happened though. She'd seen women with their breast out and sailors fondling them and couples jumping up and down together against a doorstep. She didn't think it was something to be frightened of. In fact most of them were laughing and seemed to be enjoying it.

"Yes mama," said one dutiful daughter.

***

Rose was almost a star after a few months and her wages increased by a shilling. Mr Claypole was very pleased with his little angel and the audiences loved her. It was one Saturday evening when Mr Claypole was sat at his table to the front of the house. He had a bottle of rum and a glass when a very debonair middle-aged toff sat opposite him.

"Lord Winton, welcome. We haven't seen you in these parts for a while. Please, what can I get my boy to fetch for you?"

"Hello, Claypole. I've been busy. Champagne I think and a girl if you have one."

"Always for you, sir. Always for you."

Mr Claypole signalled to one of the women at the edge of the auditorium. She snaked her way through the crowd to the table.

"Hello, my darling. Are we going to have a little fun tonight?"

She hooked her arm around the Lord's neck and whispered in his ear. They both erupted into laughter. Mr Claypole was pleased his best customer was happy.

"Who's top of the bill tonight, Claypole? Any new acts?"

Mr Claypole squirmed in his seat. He had forgotten Rose and knew the grotesque delights of Lord Winton included young children. The orchestra started with the usual drum-roll and the velvet curtains were pulled back to reveal Rose sat on her stool with her doll. She wore a pink satin dress and fur cape. The crowd roared as she sang a soulful tune, her voice as sweet as any songbird's. The crowd sang the chorus drowning out Rose as she cradled her porcelain doll to her chest.

"Claypole, where have you been hiding this sweet child?"

"She's our new act, sir. Very popular. A local lass."

"Is she available on the account Claypole?"

"No, sir. She is only a child. An innocent I'm sure."

"Yes, Claypole. Ripe for the picking. Come on, we're in Whitechapel. Everyone here has a price."

He moved the woman who was draped across him. He didn't want used goods, he wanted the doll-faced child. He drank the champagne and raised his eyebrows to Mr Claypole.

"I can ask. It's not part of her employment that she, well that she entertains privately."

"I'm not taking no for an answer man. I'm a patron of these premises. I can make you or break you. But we are friends are we not? You will not deny me."

"I'll ask her to join us, sir."

Mr Claypole didn't know what he was going to say to Rose, and he didn't know if Patrick was going to meet her after the final show. Rose was in the dressing room. She was sat in a large armchair. There was a ten o'clock show that night and supper had been sent for before reapplying her greasepaint and performing again.

"Well done my dear, well done."

He moved a chair to sit at the side of her.

"I have a gentleman, Lord Witton, who is a patron of these premises and a valued customer. He would like to meet you. He has the deepest praises for your singing and could not leave until he meets you in person. I must say, Rose, this is a very influential man and you must be very polite to him - our very existence is due to him being a generous benefactor."

Rose didn't understand why Mr Claypole would ask her to be polite. She always thought she was.

"I don't have to change from my stage clothes, do I?"

Mr Claypole shook his head. He knew that was what the Lord liked most about Rose. She tidied her hair and went to the auditorium. The Lord was sat at the table with the wench he had been given, drinking from a champagne goblet. Mr Claypole nervously sat opposite him an acrobat swung on a rope above their heads.

"Here she is, the east-end songbird herself, sweet Rosie. Come hear my dear."

He patted the chair he had just pushed the whore from.

"You are adorable my dear. I'm so sorry I missed your debut."

"Thank you, kind sir."

Rose sensed a strange tingle through her body. She felt unsafe and wanted to run from the theatre. She hoped Patrick would arrive soon. She didn't wish to be left with the gentleman. The first house finished and the rabble in the gods left. The gentlefolk were then cared for by waiters and waitresses with drinks and platters of food. Rose was invited to dine. There were oysters and plaice, pheasant and a cream pudding. Rose had never eaten such rich fayre.

Lord Witton didn't show any manners as he ate with his mouth open to reveal the meat he was chewing and he constantly pawed Rose, stroking her hair then her shoulders. Her flesh crawled in disgust.

Chapter Forty-Six

Rose felt a little woozy when she returned to the dressing room. The other performers gave her a few words of support.

"Watch him, Rose. He's a strange one," said Vincenzo the acrobat.

She smiled and thanked him for caring.

There was a call for her to go to the stage. Rose gave her face the final powder and went to start her act. Her song was more sorrowful than usual and grown men were crying in the audience. As she finished, the crowd erupted. They loved her. When she returned to the dressing room one of the ragged boys brought her a message.

"Rose, Mr Claypole wants you to go to his office straight away."

This was such an unusual event. But he was her employer. She quickly ran up the steps and knocked on the door.

"Come."

She entered. The office was dark and Mr Claypole was stood near the corner of the room. As she got closer she knew it wasn't her employer. It was Lord Witton.

"Now, my little flower, I am here to cause you no harm."

Rose ran to the door. She knew he was lying, but he was quick and stood in front of her. He locked the door and took Rose in his arms.

"Just one little kiss my Rose of Tralee."

Rose tried to wriggle free.

"Sir, please, I am an innocent. I am betrothed."

Lord Witton enjoyed this struggle more than the act itself. His breath was hot on Rose's neck and she could smell the fish he had just dined on. This made her retch and she put her hand to her mouth, enabling Lord Witton to get a firmer hold on her. He pushed her towards the desk, tearing her clothes away so he could touch her china white body, smooth as milk. Before she could scream, he entered her, pushing furiously, a shrill scream spilt from her bitten lips. The beast smothered her tiny body with hands, exploring every part of her. Rose was choking, her sobs were in vain, the pain she was experiencing was something she had never dreamt of in her darkest nightmares. When he pulled away from her, she rolled to the side and tried to cover herself.

"You've made an old man happy girl. Here you are."

He left a half a crown on the desk. Rose couldn't believe the utter disgust she felt for herself and him at that moment.

She sprang up and, with fists flying, went to beat the gentleman. He held her wrists and laughed in her face.

"What's wrong? This is the life of the music hall. You had better get used to it." He wrapped his cape around himself and put his hat on. "Madam, it has been a pleasure." He left the room laughing down the corridor.

Rose looked down and saw blood running along her bare legs and onto her white stockings, the garters still in place. Her body felt bruised inside and out. She was ashamed that she had let the man take her so easily, but he was too strong for her. She wondered if Mr Claypole had arranged for her to be part of Lord Witton's night. What would she tell Patrick? She didn't have time to think as Patrick opened the office door.

"What has happened, Rose? Tell me?" She crumpled into his arms and sobbed.

"It was Lord Witton. He attacked me. I was alone. Oh Patrick, I can't be here anymore. Please help me. He may do it again."

"He bloody well won't. Did Claypole have anything to do with this?"

"I think he might have." He thought the same as Rose.

Patrick helped her tidy herself up. She winced at the touch to her belly. It was tender because of the brutal attack.

"The bastard. I'll kill him for this, and Claypole. An innocent young woman defiled just because they have more than anyone else."

"Please take me home, Patrick."

Mr Claypole's cape was hung behind the door. He wrapped it around Rose's broken body. He couldn't look at her. He felt it was his fault not being there, not warning her of the leeches that hung around the theatre. She was ruined. No longer an innocent, he had to protect her now. When they got home, Rose's mother and father wondered what the fuss was. When they were told the tale, her father wanted to go to the police, but Patrick said it would be a waste of time. Her mother just shook her head. It happened all the time. Rose had been lucky so far in her life. She had been molested at five years old. Men were wicked in her eyes.

Chapter Forty-Seven

Patrick proved that he cared for Rose and he wanted her to live with him in rooms on Fletcher Street. Her mother and father were confident in the fact that he would look after her. She couldn't go back to the theatre. He said she could keep house and he would earn a living for both of them. The two rooms were dingy, but Rose was given money to buy net curtains and new bedding. She was happy that she didn't have to return to the place of her rape. Patrick said he would go see Mr Claypole and get her wages that she was owed. He didn't tell Rose that he also had something else on his mind. The first night in Fletcher Street was quiet. Rose had a new nightgown, a present from Patrick. She crept into the bed and waited for him to join her.

"I'm frightened, Patrick."

He stroked her hair softly. "There's no need to be frightened, my love. Close your eyes and go to sleep. I promise I'll look after you."

He couldn't make love to her. She was so delicate, like a porcelain cup. He was afraid she would break in his hands. Rose closed her eyes and nestled into Patrick's shoulder. He was her true love and she slept.

Next morning they went to the market and bought food. They watched a Punch and Judy show, then returned to their rooms. Patrick said that he had business but would be back in the afternoon. Rose busied herself, sprucing the room up, making the bed and scrubbing the floor. She was satisfied that she would make a good housewife. Patrick returned with a bunch of daisies for her. After eating Patrick said that he needed to go out again as he had to meet a man in a tavern near the river. Rose didn't mind he had to make the money for them. Patrick walked quickly to the tavern that overlooked the river. In a dark corner sat Mr Claypole. Patrick bought a glass of porter and went to sit with him.

"Patrick, so good to see you so good."

Patrick knew from the sweat on Claypole's brow he was worried.

"Did you know, Claypole, what was going to happen to Rose? Tell me, did you?"

"No, I didn't you know I loved that girl. She was like my own daughter."

"You owe her money now."

Mr Claypole reached into a velvet and leather purse he had around his middle. He laid ten shillings on the table and, with one movement, Patrick scooped them up.

"It's what she deserves. I'm sorry."

Patrick looked at him with disgust. He was aware now that Claypole had set Rose up. He drank the remnants of his glass and left. George Claypole thought he had been lucky to get away with his life.

Patrick Smith had a reputation for being a force to be reckoned with. He emptied his glass and shuffled out of the tavern and into a dark foggy night. Mother Thames was billowing her mantle across the alleyways. Mr Claypole wrapped his scarf around his neck and buried his face deep inside it. There was a footstep behind him, he turned quickly then heard a couple of sailors laugh out loud. The noise now muffled by the incoming mist. A rat ran before him making him jump. Why was he so jittery? He didn't hear the swift truncheon that hit him soundly on the back of his head, but he heard the voice in his ear.

"You are a demon, sir."

Mr Claypole couldn't speak. His throat was held firmly and his head was spinning. Blood was running into his eyes and he trembled violently.

"You allowed my Rose to become a victim. This is your

punishment."

Patrick took the purse from the old man's coat then, with one stroke, stabbed his friend in the middle of his chest. Claypole made only one sound that resembled a frog croaking. Patrick rolled the body quickly to the side of the river and kicked it over the edge. There was a splash, then nothing. Patrick looked around. He couldn't see a foot in front of him. He was alone.

He went back to his rooms to find a coal fire burning in the grate and Rose sewing by oil lamp. She was as pretty as a picture. He went across and kissed her head. She pointed to the large dark red stain.

"Patrick, you have blood on your shirt."

"Well there's a story. Look what I have."

From out of his coat he produced a small tabby cat meowing.

"Oh, she's beautiful. But the blood?"

"I had to find the cat meat man. It must have leaked from the bag."

The bag of entrails stunk the room out.

"Take it off, Patrick. I'll wash it in some milk."

When they got into bed that night, Rose cuddled up close to Patrick and he slowly kissed her lips. There was heat between them and he caressed her. Rose felt something so different from what had happened with Lord Witton. This was love. She surrendered to Patrick's needs and they fell asleep in each other's arms.

Chapter Forty-Eight

Patrick hadn't finished his revenge. He had to look for Witton. He went to the music hall. It was open and the orchestra were practising. Girls were scrubbing floors and young boys were cleaning tables.

"Hello, Maisie. Where's George?"

"Don't know, Patrick. He hasn't shown his face this morning."

Patrick spoke to a few people, one being the woman that had accompanied the Lord to a lodging house. She told Patrick that she would be meeting with him that evening and she had to find a young boy to be part of the group. His Lordship had a strange taste in his delights, but he paid well. They would start at the early show in the Music Hall then on to the Ten Bells. This was good to know, thought Patrick. It was always busy in the Bells. He may be able to distract the dirty bastard.

Patrick and Rose went to meet Rose's mother and father in the tavern. They drank a few glasses. Her parents could see their daughter was going to be all right with Patrick. He had done everything he said he would. It was too early to go home, but Patrick insisted he had work to do later that night. Rose got ready for bed. She was worried that Patrick was going to be late and that she would be alone.

"Don't be afraid, my love. I have people working for me. I have to make sure they do their deliveries you go to sleep."

He left. In his inside pocket was a long butcher's knife. He went to The Ten Bells. He couldn't see the group he had expected so he settled in the back snug and drank a large rum. The crowd in the front bar were singing and having a good time. There was a roar as a voice shouted drinks all round. Every man, woman and child tried to get to the bar shoving and pushing.

"Let his Lordship through."

The landlord wanted his best customer to get to the front so he could pay. His entourage consisted of two whores, a girl of maybe ten years old and two ragged boys of five or six. The children had barley sugars and looked as though were drunk hanging onto each other. Patrick surveyed the scene with hatred in his heart. Monsters like Witton had the money to buy whatever they wanted. That included children. Patrick's past came to haunt him and hardened his heart. He had to wait, although he just wanted to jump across the bar and beat him to a pulp.

At midnight, drinks had been flowing freely. The children of the group had settled into a corner and were sleeping. His lordship drank and mauled his companions. He then had to relieve himself. He was a little unsteady on his feet but managed to find his way through the tavern, to the backyard. There wasn't anyone in the privy, so he stood, trying to unfasten the buttons on his trousers.

"What the?"

He tried to turn around to face his attacker but couldn't. He was held in an arm-lock.

"Let me go I tell you."

Patrick took his knife and held it to Lord Witton's throat.

"You like young folk don't you, your lordship? But unfortunately you won't be able to harm another one of them."

The other man's eyes were popping from his head. He couldn't speak as he had a roll of cloth stuffed into his mouth.

"I was going to kill you. But that's too good for you."

The Lord's body seemed to relax a little. He was just

going to get robbed, he thought. Patrick unbuttoned the last two buttons of his victims' trousers and they fell to the floor. Patrick then pulled his undergarments down, so the Lord was naked from the waist down. There was now shock on Lord Witton's face. Patrick tied the Lord's hands behind him then pushed him further inside the privy. His Lordship changed the look of shock to that of horror as he realised what Patrick was about to do. He tried screaming but he was unable to let a scream escape from his stifled mouth, then he collapsed into a heap on the floor. Patrick stood up straight and held up the Lord's blood dripping penis in his hand. He threw it to the alley cats, who jumped on the fresh piece of flesh

Lord Witton was unconscious but groaning. Patrick hadn't finished. He hacked off each finger then, with a surge of strength, stabbed the dying body in the chest, finishing him off. Patrick took the money out of the gentleman's pockets and left. He had been lucky. There wasn't another soul in the backyard to disturb his actions. He was satisfied. He was now happy. He'd done what he had set out to do.

Chapter Forty-Nine

Newspaper boys on the corner of each street shouted the headlines.

"Come an' get yur news. Come an' get yur news. Lord found murdered at local tavern."

There was a buzz among the local drinking fraternity. They all knew Lord Witton. He'd spent most of his time among the vagabonds and whores of London, his money falling freely to fulfill his desires for young children. Many were pleased he had gotten his comeuppance. On the way to the market, Rose had asked one of the newsboys to let her have a quick look. Rose had mixed feelings. She was glad that Witton was dead, but she wondered who could have done it and, at the back of her mind, there was a little bell giving her the name. When Patrick arrived home at supper time, she dished his chicken stew into a bowl.

"Rose, this smells delicious. I should have known you would have been a good cook as well."

"Patrick, don't. I had to be. Mother didn't like to cook. We could have starved."

They both laughed, then Rose's face changed. The smile was gone, replaced by a furrowed brow.

"Have you heard the news?"

"That's in the papers?"

"Yes."

"About his lordship. The bastard, he got what was coming to him. I just wish I had been there. I would have put a hole in him myself."

"You didn't have anything to do with it Patrick, did you?"

He laid his spoon in his dish. "Rose, you don't think I could do that do you?"

"No of course not. But you did say you would kill him for what he had done to me."

"Calm down gal. Someone got there before me, unfortunately."

He carried on eating. Rose went to the sink and washed the pans.

Life moved on. There seemed to be a lot of police presence in the area but Lord Witton's killer was never found. Rose settled into domestic bliss. Patrick was kind and bought her small gifts. She didn't know what business he was in - he'd told her deliveries, but it could have been anything. She sometimes went to the market to sit with her mother just for some company. Patrick had started to come home very late, or on a couple of occasions he didn't come home at all. She tried to challenge him, but his mood would change, and she didn't like the other side of him.

Chapter Fifty

When Rose was a little older, her mother asked her, "Why haven't you been carrying a child?"

Rose had never thought about it. She was too busy looking after Patrick and trying to keep him sweet. She was pleased she didn't have children as things had changed in her relationship with her Irish love. Annie didn't think she was the only woman in his life, she found long brown hairs on his clothing but she dare not ask or he would have lost his temper something he had been doing on a regular basis. She knew his business was not as successful as it was, and she now realised that all Patrick did was not on the right side of the law.

"I don't know, Mama. Maybe I'm not going to have any."

That night, when Patrick came home, she gave him a supper of sausages and sat at his side, watching him eat.

"Patrick, do you want us to have a baby?"

"Bloody hell you're not pregnant are you?"

That said it all for Rose. He didn't want a child hindering him as well as her.

"No, I'm not. Are you bothered that I haven't had one."

"No, we don't want to be bringing children into this world. But if it happens, then it happens."

It wasn't what she wanted to hear. She felt the love slip out of the door.

"Do you still love me? I feel you've grown distant, that it troubles you to come home."

He threw his dish to the floor. "Can't a man have a quiet meal without a nagging woman at his ear?"

"Please. I don't know what I've done wrong."

Patrick thought she hadn't done anything wrong. It was the way he was. He was more like his father than he realised. Life was becoming difficult. He was always just an inch away from the peelers who flooded that part of London, always asking what he was doing where was he going. They knew he was up to no good but they had to catch him. Rose wasn't the innocent young girl he had met years before. She had grown fat and didn't care for herself as she used to. She had started to meet her mother at the market and after the flowers had been sold, they would frequent the taverns. Rose's father had died six months before, so Rose thought it was her duty to look after her mother and keep her company.

"You're idle Rose, out spending my money. I don't have a magic shilling tree."

"What do you want me to do? Why haven't you said before Patrick? I'll work to help you. I haven't a problem, please my love."

He realised at that moment he no longer had any desire for Rose. Her voice that he once treasured now whined at everything he did. But he felt responsible for her. He had put her in danger.

"Do what you have to do. I'm going to the tavern."

He slammed the door as he left, and Rose sat on the rag rug and cried. Patrick didn't come home that night, and in the morning he still hadn't appeared. Rose got ready and went to her mother. She cried and told her what had happened. They both went to the market together. Rose asked stall-holders if they needed help. Nobody had the need of a young woman, so she returned to be at her mother's side and became morose.

"He doesn't love me anymore," she cried.

"Don't be crying. That's what men do to you. They're always looking out for someone prettier and more pliable. You need to be looking for another yourself. Don't wait for him no more."

Rose hadn't thought about finding herself another beau. But she was getting hungry. Patrick didn't always come home. She had to eat.

The following day Patrick walked through the door as though he only gone out for a jug of milk.

"Where the hell have you been? You can't just walk in and out like this, Patrick. I need money to feed us. There isn't a thing in the cupboard. It's a good job we don't have children. They would have starved to death."

Patrick took two strides and he was at her side. He took her apron in his hands and pushed her to the wall.

"Don't speak to me when I'm the only person bringing money into this house."

He laid half a crown on the table. "Go get something to eat for us and be quick about it."

Rose picked up the money and put her bonnet on. She ran down the street calling to get a jug of milk, a loaf of bread, dripping and some sausages that had been cooked on the brazier at the end of the road.

Patrick ate his fill, not making conversation. He wiped a piece of bread around his plate, mopping up the fat.

"I feel better after that."

He seemed in a better mood, but Rose was on eggshells, not wanting to cause another outburst.

"Rose, it's not fair on you I know. I'm not myself. Things are not going as good as they should. You need to work. I can't support you any more. I can pay the rent on these rooms but everything else you need to take care of. I won't be staying anymore but I will come on a Saturday and bring your rent. I can't be fairer than that, can I?"

Rose stood with her mouth open. Fair after all she had done for him.

"You've got another woman, haven't you? I knew it, you bastard. I have given you the best years. I was always good enough when I was little Rose, but now I've grown up and can stand up for myself you don't want me."

"And out. You've grown out like a fish wife."

He found it easier to leave her if she thought badly of him.

"You bastard."

She threw the frying pan along with the fat at his head. He dodged and it hit the wall.

"Go throw yourself into the river. Don't you ever come back here."

He flew from the room, followed by a cup and the plate he had been eating from.

Chapter Fifty-One

Rose had told her mother what had happened. She wasn't surprised.

"Men have different urges than us. They can't go without sex. That's how we have the power over them. We can dangle it in front of them and they can't resist."

Rose didn't understand half of what her mother said.

"Well that didn't work with Patrick."

"That's because there was another woman dangling it in front of him, a newer fresher piece of cat meat."

"What am I going to do? There's no work around here that pays enough to put food on the table."

"There's always work for a woman in these parts."

Rose knew what her mother referred to. She shook her head. The picture of Lord Witton came into her head.

"I can't, mother."

"Of course you can. Every woman does it round here. I've had to go out myself on a few occasions in the past when your father was sick and there was no money for the rent. It's easy money. All them sailors and soldiers with fat purses wanting someone to talk sweet to. Most of the time they just want a quick kiss and a cuddle. What makes you so proud?"

Rose couldn't answer. She was in so much shock that her own mother had been a prostitute, and that her father had condoned it.

That evening they went to The Cock and drank porter. She wasn't in any mood for drink but what did she have to go home for? Rose was wondering what she could afford to eat that night when a drunken sailor sat on the stool at the side of her. The other sailors made rude comments and the man reached out and planted a kiss on Rose's cheek. She jumped up and slapped him soundly on his face.

The inn was in uproar, the poor man laid like a dead body. His crew members all laughed, the women in the tavern cheered that at least one of theirs had hit back. And, for once in a long time, Rose laughed. One of the sailors bought her gin and she threw it to the back of her throat, then another, then another. The crowd sang and Rose danced, her mother claiming her daughter had been on the stage.

It was midnight when Rose thought she had better to return home. Her mother was nowhere to be seen. She had had her fill of the drink and could just walk without keeling over.

"Come on Rose. Let a poor sailor boy help you along."

Rose thought he was a handsome sole, and they linked arms.

"And do you want some chestnuts?"

The chestnut man filled a three-cornered bag with the sweet-smelling delights and Rose and her man swayed together to her rooms. They got to a dark alley and the sailor pushed Rose into a shop doorway. He kissed her roughly.

"Steady on."

She pushed him backwards trying to focus on her admirer.

"Come on gal. Don't be difficult."

He tried to lift her skirts and it then dawned on her what was about to happen.

"Oh no. I didn't. I wasn't."

But it was too late. He pushed her to the door and lifted her skirts up and thrust himself into her. The act took two minutes and he drew away, leaving a mentally-scarred Rose. She had relived her ordeal with Lord Witton, but it was over, and she was still alive. The sailor went into his pocket and pulled out a shilling.

"Here you go pretty Rose. We ain't all monsters you know."

She realised that and saying goodbye. She took her shilling to the hot food stalls and bought her supper. Perhaps her mother was right. Maybe this occupation could work for her.

Chapter Fifty-Two

Monday August 6th, 1888

In the Tavern that night Rose had a strange feeling. There was a tension in the air that she hadn't experienced before. Two men at the bar were facing the crowd with their backs against the brass rail. The tallest was dressed well for a local man and the smaller one the same with a grand brushed hat with a feather in the side. They looked at the girls that Rose was sat with, undressing them with their eyes.

Rose drank her gin and left with a shiver down her back. She hadn't got very far when a young soldier asked her if she wanted to earn sixpence.

"You don't get much for sixpence. Let's see the colour of your money."

The man handed over a silver sixpence and Rose secreted it into her bodice. They went into the yard at St George's buildings and found a dark doorway. The business was over and done within two minutes. Rose wiped herself with her flannel petticoat and pulled her clothes into place. She called at the hot potato man for her supper and wandered back to her mother's.

***

The following morning, she strolled onto Whitechapel High Street. The sun was shining and there were people rushing about their daily business. The newspaper boy at the corner of the street had a crowd around him.

"Murder in Whitechapel. Get your paper. Murder in Whitechapel."

Money was exchanged for a copy of The London Daily Post. Rose wasn't going to buy a paper but stood with a woman she knew and read the grim news. A woman had been found in St George's Yard with vicious stab wounds. There was a monster living among them. Rose put her hand to her throat. It was the same yard she went to the night before with her sixpenny beau. It could have been her, could it have been the soldier she was with.

Her mother had more information from the market. The woman was Martha Tabram. She had terrible stab wounds to her body.

"You need to be careful, Rose. That Martha was selling herself. You never know who's dallying with you."

Her mother was right as usual, but she needed the money. She wasn't fit to do anything else.

"I'll be careful mother. I promise."

Chapter Fifty-Three

Thursday 30th August, 1888

Rose bought a new bonnet from the pawn brokers on Commercial Road. It had beautiful satin ribbons which she fastened into a great bow beneath her chin.

"Well you look the lady in that my love."

Kind words from her mother made her feel easier to go out and earn her crust.

The tavern was full, and the mood was a good one. In one corner there were almost a dozen women who earned their living through prostitution. They were friends and often helped each other if there was a need. They were strong women together and their language would make a sailor blush. As music hall comics, they made fun of the men in the bar, but everyone enjoyed the banter. Rose recognised the two men at the end of the bar, one tall, one shorter, both full of their own importance. Polly went to the taller of the two.

"Hello handsome. Would you like to buy a lady a little gin?"

The tall man showed a set of tombstone teeth.

"I'd be happy to when I see a lady."

The group of women made cackling sounds.

The other man smiled "I'll buy all of you pretty women a drink. Landlord, please, gins around for the bevy of beauties."

The women cheered and two took hold of the shorter man's arms

"Steady ladies. These arms have special work to do. Me and my good friend here work at the hospital."

There was an audible hum. The woman drank their glasses of gin. Rose tipped the glass in one gulp. A sailor stood by her side and asked her to accompany him into the back yard. After a quick discussion on a price, they left to complete the deal. When she returned ten minutes later, most of the women had gone, all earning their own supper. She had a couple of other customers then decided she would go home. The tavern trade had gone quiet and if she had another drink she didn't think she would be able to walk.

Friday 31st August

"Read all about it. Read all about it."

There was an excitement on the street. Her mother's next-door neighbour had said there had been another murder. Rose got dressed and ran to the tavern. Her group of friends was already there, each with glasses of drink.

"Oh, Rose, its Polly. She's been murdered like the other one. Brutally murdered slashed open." She sat down and took a drink from the table and took a mouthful.

"Who could have done such a thing? She was so lovely. She always helped out."

The sad throng reminisced and drank more gin.

"We have to keep safe, girls. We need to look out for each other."

Rose tried to uplift the women who were now sobbing into each other's laps.

"We need to earn a crust, Rose."

"I know we do, but be careful where you take em. Go where others can hear you. If you shout, tell people where you are going. We've got to stick together."

The women nodded in agreement. For the next few days there was an excitement in the taverns. People had flocked to

Whitechapel to see where the bodies had been found. Rose thought they were gruesome, but she had made a few pennies showing people the sites of the two murdered women.

The peelers were everywhere. Rose felt safer than before. No murderer would chance another brutality with the police on every corner.

Chapter Fifty-Four

Saturday 8th September, 1888

The whole of Whitechapel took to the streets.

Rose's mother was screaming about the house.

"Rose, Rose. There's been another killing. Please, God, have mercy on us."

They wandered into the street. Newspaper boys were doing a roaring trade and there were some warehouse men stood on the corner of the street, one on the top of a fruit box.

"Ladies and Gentlemen, we need to ask the police what they are doing about keeping our women safe so they can go about their daily business without getting murdered. Who's with me? Let's go to Leman Street Police station."

His hand went into the air calling all to his rally. It was excitement for Rose and her mother. They moved along with the ever-increasing crowd. Carriages weren't able to move as the mob descended on Leman Street.

The leaders didn't go into the police station, but the fruit box was placed on the pavement and the tall man wearing a large drivers hat led the chanting crowd.

"We want answers. What do we want?"

The crowd answered.

After ten minutes an inspector came out of the building and spoke with clarity.

"You all need to go home and look after your women folk. We'll get this fiend. If you have any information, come in and tell my Sergeant. If you haven't, kindly move on or you will be arrested."

Most of the men scuffed their shoes on the pavement and moved away, but the leader went inside to carry on his barrage of insults to the police. Rose and her mother walked back towards home, stopping off at the Tavern with neighbours to take a drop of mother ruin.

"Why ain't no one seen them? Somebody must have seen em."

Her mother took a deep gulp of the gin.

"It's a tragedy."

The crowd fell into a morbid rant. They heard that their leader, one Albert Porter, had been arrested for inciting the riot.

"Quick to arrest someone they have on their bleeding doorstep."

Rose and her mother linked arms and swayed all the way home.

***

It was a few days before Rose tried to get a customer. She had a feeling of foreboding. However, her stomach ensured that she went back to work without it. She and her mother would starve otherwise. She had noticed that a lot of the toffs didn't stay late in Whitechapel anymore, so her custom came from soldiers and sailors. She was still able to attract a lad or two. They wanted a good time and she was able to give them one. She often sang in the tavern. It seemed to attract a steady stream of willing participants.

At the bar were two odd gents. Someone had told her they were mortuary assistants at Old Montague Street workhouse. That explained it they were like the living dead. Robert Mann looked at his friend.

"What's up with you, James? You've a face like a mile of tripe."

His friend stared into his ale.

"James, I thought you'd be in a favourable mood. We've been able to clear this city of vermin. That's what we set out to do, didn't we?"

James nodded. Yes, they'd been busy, and he had enjoyed every last minute of it. The sharp intake of breath when the knife cut into the soft flesh gave him a feeling he had almost forgotten and the tearing of skin like gutting a rabbit when he was a boy. Robert enjoyed the sexual arousal he got from the killings, but his pleasure was for his mind, the petrified victim gave off a scent that oozed through his veins it gave him strength. It fed him. And there were so many more. He turned to listen to the little canary singing for her supper.

Chapter Fifty-Five

Saturday 29th September, 1888

Rose's mother had been unable to go to the market that day. She was suffering from a bad case of dropsy. Rose took her basket and the shilling she had for flowers. After going to the wholesale market, she set up her pitch. They couldn't not go. Crowds were descending into the area, the local people were like animals in a zoo.

Rose had sold her basket full by two o'clock in the afternoon. She bought hot sausages and boiled onions for them both and a jug of rice milk to mix with some arrowroot for her mother.

"I don't know what I would do without you my dear. That Patrick did me a favour he did."

Rose wasn't too sure, but she looked after her mother. If they didn't have the two wages coming into the house they would lose the roof over their heads, probably ending up in the workhouse. She ensured her mother had eaten and made her some more arrowroot and milk, then put some kindling in the grate to take away the dampness from the room.

"I'm going to The Cock mother. I'll take the big jug and fetch you a gill of ale for your supper."

Her mother nodded and went back to sleep. The tavern was lively regardless of there being a monster running loose on London Town.

"Here's Rose. How's your mother, Rose?"

She assured everyone that her mother was on the road to recovery and should be back to work in a day or two.

Albert Porter was at the bar. He had been released from jail that morning with a two-shilling fine. He told the working girls that the men in the area would look out for them. Robert Mann and James Hatfield joined in with the same sentiments. The women were filled with confidence that, while they were selling their wares, their protectors were in ear shot. Rose had her fill of gin. She had lifted her petticoat three times that night and earned herself one and sixpence, which wasn't bad.

She spent a penny on ale for her mother and took a leisurely stroll home trying to keep to the gas lit streets. The mist had started to swirl creeping over the pavement and cobbles footsteps echoed now and Rose felt a chill crawl over her body. She gave a shiver and drew her shawl around her.

A clip clopping of a horse and cart joined her footsteps. The two men sat on the driver's seat went passed the horse snorted in the cool air. She quickened her pace not wanting to spill her precious ale. Her mother was awake and looked a little better the arrowroot easing her kidneys.

"Oh, you've brought me ale. Lovely. Just what I need. Come and tell me what has happened. Have they caught the beast?"

Rose told her mother the tales from the tavern then took her skirt and bodice off and climbed into bed with the old woman. Both went to sleep not knowing that in Dutfield's yard, Lizzie Stride was having her throat cut by an unnamed assailant.

***

At the market the next day, as Rose bought her flowers, the news that another murder had taken place ran like wildfire through the streets. The Queen herself had spoken to the police and told the Prime Minister that no stone was to be left unturned in the search for the murderer. Her mother made a remarkable recovery, eager to be on the streets to hear the news. A ripple of excitement, fear and anger had alighted the East End of London. Police swamped the area, usually two manned. They would stroll with their arms behind their backs, watching and arresting anyone who they thought was suspicious.

Rose had become close friends with a Henry Parker. He knew she was a whore and he didn't care. She felt a little safer that she had a man who could look after her. He was kind-hearted, he didn't want a share of her earnings and bought her the occasional present - a hair comb or glass beads. Her mother didn't care so long as Rose brought home the money to her.

Chapter Fifty-Six
Friday 9th November, 1888

The horrific murder of Mary Kelly stunned the community. The ferocity with which the murderer had inflicted the brutal injuries were beyond the comprehension of many. Pictures and artist drawings were distributed among every tavern and inn across the town. They showed what was left of the pretty young girl, her face torn with her nose missing, her torso opened wide with parts of her organs missing. It was though a wild animal had savaged her. Rose had known Mary. She had often joined her in singing to the tavern - a lively girl, and now dead in her own room, on her own bed. Rose drowned her sorrows in a large glass of gin.

The men of the borough joined forces and rallied outside of the police station, to show the establishment that the workers and residents of the East End of London had had their fill of poverty and murder. A few men with top hats and dress coats stood on the back of carts and told the mobs that all was being done as could be. There had been a number of arrests, but all had been released days later, usually with broken jaws and black eyes in an attempt to get a confession out of them. Churches and chapels opened their doors at night to allow vulnerable women to take shelter, although those doing so had to accept to pay by sharing prayers and confessions.

Wednesday 19th December

Rose walked with her mother to the market. She helped her fill the basket with garlands of holly and mistletoe. You could smell the gingerbread already in the bakers' shops. The chestnut man was doing a roaring trade. Rose tossed her chestnut from one hand to the other trying not to burn her fingers. The taste was divine, and the nut melted in her mouth.

They left the market, and Rose told her mother she would come back with a treat of sausage and a jug of ale later that night. She had a glass of gin in the first tavern she came too and exchanged the general gossip with a few women. There wasn't a ship moored up on the Thames so she hoped there would be a group of soldiers from the barracks about a little later. It was almost eight o'clock in the evening when she was walking on Poplar High Street. She recognised James Hatfield and Robert Mann dressed in sombre outfits as though they had been to a funeral.

"Good evening to you, mistress. Look James, it's our little canary. Are you selling your wares tonight? You have two eager souls here that need a taste of a young woman."

"No, I am not in the mood to sell anything, especially to you grim pair."

"Come mistress, we have ready money - two shillings and a glass of porter, if you desire to have a glass with us before business."

"No, No."

Rose escaped from the duo, side-stepping to make away before the tall one made a grab for her. She ran towards The George and Commercial Road. She felt ill. The two had given her a fright. If anyone was guilty of murder, it would have been them. In the George she managed to earn three shillings. Unfortunately she drank almost a shilling on gin. Her friend Lizzie had borrowed sixpence to get a bed in a doss house for the night, but she didn't mind. They weren't as lucky as she was living with her mother. She also bought

Lizzie her supper. They dined on meat and potatoes that the landlord's wife had made.

"You don't have to buy me food, Rose. You've given me enough."

"You never know when I might need the favour, Lizzie. We gals need to stick together."

Chapter Fifty-Seven

Thursday 20th December, 1888

It was half past two in the morning when the crowd in the George quietened down. Rose thought it best to go home while she could still stand. The roads were crisp with frost and she pulled her jacket around her body. There was a cough in the sharp air and Rose turned around expecting to see someone behind her but there was no one there. As she walked along Poplar High Street, close to Clarke's Yard, a cart and two men sat on the driver's seat came towards her. She was thankful there were still people about. The horse clipped slowly and without warning a cord was placed around her neck and pulled tight. Rose tried to get her fingers in between her neck and the cord. She couldn't breathe and her feet left the ground, her struggles were short-lived as a stream of blood fell from her nose.

A voice from above shouted down to the yard.

"Who's that, I say? Who's down there?"

Footsteps, then nothing. Rose lay life extinguished.

The two mortuary assistants touched their glasses. The tavern was full of women and men swilling ale down. Two women arguing over a red ribbon.

"Women are the devil, James. Even those that sing like angels."

***

4:15am

Sergeant Robert Goulding found the body of Rose Mylett in Clarke's Yard. The woman's body was still warm when found and positioned like previous ripper victims.

***

Inquest Led by Wynne Baxter.
Inquest findings murder by person or persons unknown.
The body was found only two miles from Whitechapel.
The deceased was wearing:
Brown and Black clothing,
Dark tweed jacket,
Lilac apron,
Red flannel petticoat,
Red and blue stripped stockings,
She had a half penny on her person.

Author's Note

My passion for the enigma of Jack the Ripper has led me to write about other murders that were not accredited to him in the year 1888. The four stories are fictional stories intertwined with a few true events. The women lived and died in Whitechapel London 1888. The police at that time did not believe that they were victims of Jack the Ripper but never found any other assailant. I have my own idea who were responsible for the murders and there is a thread through the four stories.

There have been many interpretations of who Jack the Ripper was and who his victims were. This is my perception of what happened in Whitechapel at the end of the century.

Emma Smith was reported to have a refined cultured voice. Her story is the downwards spiral of a life taken from wealth and luxury to the grime and filth of London town. Her struggles and heartbreaks echo the lives of most women living and working in Whitechapel in that era.

Martha Taubram was born in London who from an early age enjoyed being part of the underclass, drinking and selling her body for a few pennies. She married and could have accepted a comfortable life with a husband and children. However, the draw of mother's ruin(gin) was too much for her and she joined the homeless and criminal class.

Annie Miller widowed and had very little opportunities to escape the pit of poverty. Her life led her to murder having experienced domestic violence that was part of everyday life in Victorian times. Her sad tale and untimely death is a chilling memory of what life could have been like. Struggling to find a crust to eat and only one step away from the workhouse, she has to come to a decision that is alien to her.

Catherine (Rose)Mylett (Millett) was described as fair of face. Blonde and a pale complexion. My story takes you to the popular Music Halls that entertained the rich and the poor. Her story has been connected to that of Emma Smith by an Irish rogue Patrick Smith.

Fantastic Books
Great Authors

darkstroke is
an imprint of
Crooked Cat Books

- Gripping Thrillers
- Cosy Mysteries
- Romantic Chick-Lit
- Fascinating Historicals
- Exciting Fantasy
- Young Adult and Children's Adventures
- Non-Fiction

Discover us online
www.darkstroke.com

Find us on instagram:
www.instagram.com/darkstrokebooks

Printed in Great Britain
by Amazon